A CUT ABOVE

Memoirs of God's Favorite Barber

Thomas Barillier

A CUT ABOVE

Memoirs of God's Favorite Barber

First Edition, 2021
Digital Edition, 2021

Distributed by:

Ingram Book Group, LLC
One Ingram Boulevard
La Vergne, Tennessee 37086
615-793-5000
www.ingramspark.com

ISBN: 978-0-9967839-1-0

Book Graphic Design and Layout: Andrew Alfe

To my daughter Charlotte.

It's said a father's job is to teach a child by example,
but throughout our lives, it was, more often you
that taught me in the most innocent way.
This book is my legacy to you and the key
to understanding your father.
I hope you enjoy it,
but more importantly, I hope, through the years,
it will bring many happy memories.

With all my love, Dad

Acknowledgments:

A special thank you to Fred Freeman, Bob Gale, Stu Kreiger, Jeff Melvoin, Mathew Tekulsky, and the late great Lorenzo Sample Jr., for helping make the dream of writing this book a reality. Your advice, encouragement, and mentoring helped keep me moving forward.

And, thank you to two very special and talented women, Lisa Flowers and Glendle McPherson. You are my muses… my daughters of Zeus and Mnemosyne. This book would never have been completed, if not for your inspiration, your suggestions, and your steadfast belief in me during times when I found it hard to believe in myself.

Finally, thanks to Andrew Alfe for getting into the mud and doing all the dirty work so necessary to bring the book to the shelf. Your expertise made the process seamless allowing me to focus on writing.

A note from the author...

Without questions, there would be no answers, yet most of mankind fear the question as much as they fear the serpent. As a child, I was raised by parents who taught me to embrace the power of questions and the inevitability that they will create more new questions than answers. As the years passed, I found that to be the only truth.

This story is not about God, The Bible, or religion. It's about questions and provides no answers. It's not intended to change minds, nor does it support any path to enlightenment. I leave that to the reader. All I ask is that those who read it ask their own questions and not from any preconceived prejudices.

Chapter I

It wasn't just another day –
it was my last day.

When I woke up that morning, the air was fresh and filled with the anticipation of my pending adventure. Over the last few years, my motivation to cut hair, like my scissors, had become dull and my love for the smell of bay rum had been replaced by the warm salty scent of the sea. While most people my age were busy winding down, I was getting ready to ramp up, and like my favorite author, Mark Twain, once wrote, "The time had come to throw off the bowlines and catch the trade winds in my sails."

Speaking of writing, over the last few years, I had developed a passion for the written word. It didn't matter to me if I was any good; I just thought it would be fun to write about all those interesting, clever, and sometimes crazy people that had sat in my barber chair through the years. People like "Crazy" Dick, who always brought with him a pocketful of humorous quips that would bring tears of laughter to everyone's eyes. Or Stewart, whose one claim to fame was his impersonation of the horn on a VW minibus. There was Tim, the self-proclaimed princess of Malibu who once wore the same coat to a party that my friend's wife wore, and Blaine, who was so right-wing that in the Truman / Dewey election, I'm sure he voted for Himmler.

There were also interesting patrons. Simon, who was a Holocaust survivor that became Einstein's assistant, and Rube, who went from a farm boy in the central valley to one of the most influential aerospace engineers of the twentieth century. Of course, there were all the doctors, lawyers, CEOs, writers, and educators that frequented my chair. I was blessed to have such interesting customers, and they made cutting hair more than just a job; it was a never-ending institution of higher learning.

With all due respect to the great teachers in my life, I learned more standing behind that barber chair than I ever learned sitting at a desk. If I had a question on any subject, I was confident that someone in the next couple of weeks would sit in my chair with the answer. Even if I had no questions, spending a half-hour (or so) every month with these men opened my eyes to a world beyond my barbershop, and what better way to write down all these experiences, than sitting on the deck of my new boat, with a glass of wine in hand, looking out at the horizon?

Don't get me wrong – it wasn't that I suddenly hated barbering. Life as a barber was easy in its neat little box. I would go to work, make a little money, go out and have some fun, come home, go to bed, get up, and do it all over again. It never occurred to me I could have done anything more gratifying in my life than watching young men grow up to be fathers and their sons grow up to become young men. Life was pretty simple as a barber, but now, it was time to vault over the side of that neat little box and run at the sun.

Yeah, it was my last day, but it was also my first day, and the first act of this new day was to deep-six all devices with a common denominator of twenty-four. Time was about to become a four-letter word. The house was sold, the money was safely stashed away, and all that was left was to walk out of my barbershop for the last time and onto the deck of my single mast, floating piece of Heaven called A Cut Above.

When I announced my last day at the shop, many of my customers, showing their appreciation for my years of loyalty, arrived to shower me with cards, gifts, and well wishes. One of them even brought a huge balloon in the shape of a ship that said, "Bon Voyage" on one side, and "Good Luck" on the other. I never thought of myself as a sentimental guy, but I had to admit, those mementos meant a lot to me and would remain fond memories that I planned on carrying with me for the rest of my life. So, I loaded them into the back seat of my car, dropped the keys to the shop through the mail slot in the door, and drove away for the last time.

As I drove, I pondered where this new adventure would lead me. Over the years, I had spent many an idle moment between haircuts imagining adventures to the far corners of the world like a Walter Mitty dream, with a saber in one hand and a beautiful maiden in the other. I was still fairly young, still healthy, and felt the passion a young man felt as he set out in search of his prize. I was about to become an albatross at the mercy of the wind, with a destination as far away as that wind would take me.

If only my car had been as vibrant, the outcome might have been different, but the years had caught up to it and its life seemed to be failing with every turn of the key. I had avoided buying a new car because it made no sense to spend good money on something I would soon have no use for. Fortunately, my mechanic, being the magician he was, had managed to keep me on the road for the last few months. But my car was like an aging horse that should have been put to pasture long ago. The engine sounded like a lawnmower, and the air conditioning – when it worked – was like someone blowing their warm breath in my face.

It was a hotter than usual day for that time of the year, but since I was driving along the coast, I could lower the windows to help keep cool. As I approached my favorite watering hole, my temptation to stop and cool off for one last toast while saying goodbye to my favorite cutie of a bartender was overruled by my excitement to begin this new adventure. So, as I passed by, I looked over one last time and with a smile on my face, gave a two-finger salute goodbye.

When I looked back to the highway, a car that had been parked on the side of the road had suddenly come out right in front of me, cutting me off. Fortunately, my reflexes were still pretty quick, and I managed to avoid impending doom, but then I found myself on the wrong side of the road.

As I saw cars approaching me from the other direction, frantically honking their horns, I managed to maneuver back to my side of the highway with a quick jerk of the wheel, but that quick turn had stirred the mementos in my back seat and suddenly something was blocking my view of the road.

All I remember after that was the sound of shattering glass and crushing metal. I could hear voices calling to me, but I was unable to respond as the car filled with water. The initial panic as I gasped for breath was quickly replaced with a calming sensation. I don't know if it was because I had succumbed to the reality of my fate, or the acceptance of the passing from life to death, but a sense of peace came over me.

The next thing I knew, I was standing in a long line of people in what looked like a DMV office. By the time my head began to clear, I was at the front of the line, and on the other side of the counter was a man, with the voice of a Brooklyn bus driver, asking me my name.

A bit dazed and confused, I replied, "Barry, Barry Masters. Where am I?"

Rather than answering my question, he became excited. He turned to the man working next to him and said, "Barry's here, he's finally here. Go get the boss, quick!"

In a tone of confusion, I asked again. "Where am I?"

While still looking back for the boss, he tossed over his shoulder, "You're in Heaven!"

My head was still in a fog when I asked, "Heaven? What do you mean, Heaven?"

With a blend of annoyance and sarcasm in his voice, he repeated, "Heaven... H-E-A-V-E-N. You know, like 'Stairway to.'" Then he turned around and looking at me said, "Ya know, we've been waiting for you for what seems like an eternity."

Another guy standing next to him started laughing. "Eternity, good one!"

They both laughed and he continued, "We've been waiting for you for so long and The Big Kahuna can get pretty impatient. And when he does...let's just say, it ain't no picnic for the rest of us."

I began to feel a bit of anger brewing inside, and with the little patience I had, I asked, "What's your name?"

"Marvin," he replied.

As calmly as I could, considering the circumstances, I said, "Okay, Marvin, can you understand that I'm feeling a bit confused here, so please help me. If this is Heaven, how the hell did I get here?"

Marvin: "Let me look and see."

He opened a big book like he was investigating my question, but I got the feeling he already knew.

Marvin: "Well, remember the car that cut in front of you to make the U-turn?"

Barry: "Ahh...so I hit it?"

Marvin: "Naw, you missed it, but to avoid hitting it, you had to swerve across the center line."

Barry: "Oh...so I hit another car head-on?"

Marvin: "Nope, you managed quite well to get back to your side of the road."

Barry: "So, how the hell did I get here?"

Marvin: "Well, remember the 'Bon Voyage' balloon in your back seat? Well, it turned out to be good luck for us, not you."

Just then, an older balding man with a really bad combover haircut approached us and with a soothing voice introduced himself, "So, you're Barry. I'm Peter. How are you?" With the muscles in my face as tightly drawn as a rubber band about to snap, I took a deep breath.

Barry: "Not good. This guy is telling me I'm in Heaven? What kinda crap is that?"

Peter just smiled and with that same calming voice said, "Well, everyone is excited you're finally here. Welcome to Heaven, Barry."

In a voice that could best be described as annoyed and desperate.

Barry: "Heaven? But this isn't fair. I spent my whole life sacrificing everything for my one little dream and you just ripped it away from me."

Peter: "Fair schmair! That was never your destiny."

My tone of annoyance and desperation turned

back to anger as I snapped.

Barry: "Destiny? I don't give a crap about my destiny."

Peter snapped back: "Maybe you don't, but he does, and that's all that matters."

Even more confused than when this conversation began.

Barry: "Who is this 'he' you guys keep talking about...God?"

Peter smiling: "Of course."

.Barry:" What does He care whether I live or die?"

Peter: "Simple, He needs a haircut, and you're His favorite barber."

Although I was flattered, none of what Peter was saying made sense.

Barry: "You mean, in all of Heaven, I'm the only good barber?"

Peter looked over at his compatriots and chuckled,

Peter: "No, there are lots of good barbers here, but He wants you."

As a rule, I try to avoid confrontation, but I could no longer continue to bite my lip

Barry: "Well, what if I don't want to cut His hair?"

Peter: "God, Barry... God. That's with a capital G. Do you really think you're gonna win this one?"

Unfortunately, I knew he was right, but my mind

began to reflect on all those sacrifices I had made throughout my life for my one little dream, and it was about to be blown out of the water on a whim of the Almighty. Then, I remembered what a customer once told me: don't waste a moment concerning yourself over things you can't change.

So, resigning to this reality, I thought, Maybe they have oceans here I could sail on when I'm not cutting His hair.

Barry: "Got any oceans up here?"

Peter: "Not a one,"

Barry: "How 'bout lakes?"

Peter With little interest in continuing this conversation: "Nope."

Barry: "Well, what do you have that a sailor like me could enjoy?"

Peter: "We have a barbershop."

It became as clear as a calm lagoon that I had lost this fight.

Barry: "Okay, so what do I do now?"

Peter: "Follow me."

Chapter II

It was a short walk to the shop. As we approached, I could see on the window in gold leaf, "A Cut Above," and underneath the name, in smaller letters, it read "God's Favorite Barber" with my name as the proprietor at the bottom of the window. I thought to myself, Woe! what an endorsement! God's Favorite Barber?

Peter opened the door and gestured for me to go in. I had to admit, it was a great shop. There were two big, comfy, vintage mid-century barber chairs and the finest tools money could buy. Across from the mirrors was a giant flat-screen TV playing the World Series. I had always wanted a shop like this. In fact, I wanted this exact shop, but it always seemed like such a waste of money that could be better spent on my dream.

Oh yeah, my dream... I had almost forgotten about it. I began to think again how unfair all this was when Peter came in.

Barry: "So, where is He?"

Peter: "He'll be here soon, but before He comes, could you give me a trim?"

With an apathetic shrug, I agreed. I wrapped him up, and with the curiosity that had been my trademark on Earth, started asking him questions.

Barry: "So, your name's Peter?"

Peter: "Yep."

Barry: "As in Saint Peter?"

Peter: "The same."

Barry: "Should I just call you Peter?"

Peter: "Please!"

Barry: "So, Peter, who's been cutting your hair?"

Peter: "Oh, some guy on the other side of Heaven."

Barry: "What did he do that you didn't like?"

Peter: "Nothing, he did a good job."

Barry: "Then why not go back to him?"

Peter: "Because you're God's favorite barber. That means you're the best."

I thought to myself, Great...now I'm the best. For forty years, I was just another barber in West Los Angeles. Never got any more than four stars on

Yelp and now, when it was the last thing I wanted, I was the best? Of course, I guess there could be worse things than being God's favorite barber, but why me? Why did God pick me? I had a thousand questions and only one extremely bald man to ask. I combed through his hair while making sure to keep the questions coming.

Barry: "So, are you the guy that gives the thumbs up or down as far as who gets in here?"

Peter: "Well, I ask the questions and do the research, but God makes the final decision. A lot of the time, if it was up to me, I'd say no, but then, out of the blue, He hits the thumbs-up button and who's gonna argue, right? I wish there was a direct set of rules, but the whole process is pretty subjective and based on His whims."

Barry: "Does that happen a lot?"

Peter: "More than you would think. You'd be surprised who is here and who isn't. I know I am. Most people on Earth think a couple of prayers, a little praise, and sacrificing one day of their week is enough to get them in God's good graces, but it takes a lot more than that. Truth be told, He doesn't care about prayers or praises and never listens to them. He's kind of an 'action over words' guy."

Barry: "Really? You know, I never gave much stock in that praying thing either. It seems to me that most people only pray because they want something, but if it's true He doesn't listen, where did the whole praying thing come from?"

Peter: "Well, things were tough after Jesus was crucified. The people were abandoning the flock in every direction. So, those of us who followed Jesus were desperate and decided we had to do something. First, we decided we needed to tell his story the best we could. The problem was that we all had different versions of what his story should be. We decided it would be good to pull all our memories together in a new book and call it the New Testament. The first few chapters were easy. They were letters Paul had written to spread the faith throughout the Mediterranean world. It got a lot harder after that, especially since none of us could read or write. The rest came over the next couple of centuries and most of it was written by future generations of followers."

Barry: "So, most of it is a fraud?"

Peter: "That's a bit harsh. I'd rather think of it like that game, Telephone. You know, where there is a line of people and a person at one end whispers a message to the person next to them, and by the time it gets to the other end, it's completely different. We all remembered it differently and no one could agree on what actually happened."

Barry: "So, who decided what would be in it and

what wouldn't?"

Peter: "King James, but I guess the best answer to that question is no one because there are over forty-five thousand denominations around the world, and every one of them tells a different story."

Barry: "Sounds like the most elaborate game of Telephone in the history of man."

Peter didn't have much hair, and I was running out of things to do, but I still wanted an answer to my original question.

Barry: "But what about praying?"

Peter: "Praying is as old as man himself. Cavemen prayed, the Egyptians, Greeks, and Persians all prayed. Every civilization prayed. Paul the Apostle took it to the next level. He was a brilliant marketing guy, and used it as a great marketing tool. He figured if just one out of a million prayers appeared to be answered even though it was nothing more than coincidence, everyone would think all their prayers would be answered. And when the majority weren't answered, the excuse would be that God had another plan for them. Of course, God doesn't have the time or the inclination to answer all the prayers and He has no plan for every single person, especially when there are so many planets all praying at the same time. Oh, by the way, you do know Earth is not the only planet with intelligent life in the universe?"

Barry: "I figured there were other planets with life, but I didn't know for sure. I guess you could call me an alien agnostic."

Peter laughed and said, "Common sense would tell you there must be. You lived near the beach, right? Imagine all those grains of sand and just one on your little toe is the only grain, in the world, that has life. No way, no how. Although, I will say Earth is His favorite, even though it needs the most attention."

I was worried about cutting his hair too short, but this conversation was great, and I didn't want it to end.

Barry: "I'm curious. Does God want us to be afraid of Him? I've always been troubled by the "fear of God" thing. Seems to me that if we are His children, that's not very good parenting. I mean… I wouldn't want my children to be afraid of me."

Peter: "Truth be told, God's not scary at all. He's not all that different from you and me. Yeah, He can get mad and on occasion jealous, but He also loves, and most of all, loves to laugh."

Barry: "So, what makes Him laugh?"

Peter: "He has a very dry sense of humor. I would say, the human obsession with sex will always bring out a big laugh."

Barry: "So, what else can I expect when he comes for his haircut?"

Peter: "He's quiet. Only speaks when He has something to say and since He's God, He usually doesn't have much to say. You'll like Him I'm sure. He has a real interest in all of us…even though He doesn't get involved in our daily lives."

I had run out of hair to cut, so it seemed to be a good time to change the conversation and ask the most important question.

Barry: "So, how do you like your haircut?"

He looked for a long moment in the mirror and said, "I love it, but that's not a surprise. After all, you're God's favorite barber, right?"

A chill came over me again. I'm God's favorite barber? That was certainly what it said on the window, but once again I thought, how would He know I was the best? After all, I had never cut His hair. My mind began to jump from one thought to another. Maybe I'm sleeping and all this is a dream. Maybe this isn't as bad as I think. After all, God's favorite barber sounded awfully cool. But what if God didn't like me or His haircut? What would happen to me? Would I be shipped off to the other place? What would it be like there? Or, maybe He did like it and my reward would be that I'd be sent back to Earth after His haircut and go back to my dream. My thoughts were traveling at the speed of light when Peter repeated himself.

Peter: "Barry? Are you okay? I said I think it looks great."

I returned to the moment.

Barry: "I'm sorry! I was a million miles away. I'm glad you like it. The first thing I did was to get rid of that combover. You weren't fooling anyone. What you should be trying to do is to change the focus from the top of your head down to your eyes."

Peter smiled. "That makes sense. You're pretty good at this."

I smiled back.

Barry: "I should be; I'm God's favorite barber, right?"

Peter: "For now you are, but don't get cocky about it. He can turn on a dime. Look at Lucifer. He was God's favorite angel. He was beautiful, but he was too independent. Of course, God made him that way by giving him free will, but then got angry when he tried to express it."

Barry: "But isn't he evil?"

Peter: "Not at all. Don't tell God I said this, but Lucifer was merely using that free will God gave him. When He threw Lucifer out of Heaven, we all learned quickly that using our free will was like walking on a pond of thin ice."

Barry: "So, Satan's not responsible for all the evil in the world?"

Peter: "Hell no! Man only has himself to blame

for all that evil. Humans aren't victims, but good luck convincing them. They don't want it better; they just want it easier and Lucifer was the perfect scapegoat. He's actually a very sweet creature. The Lucifer in the Bible was created by man to avoid taking responsibility."

On that comment, I decided I had better stop asking questions and do the final touches on his haircut. It didn't take long to finish, and as I removed the chair cloth, I asked him again if he liked it. He responded with an emphatic yes!

Even though I was still a bit angry at my situation, I smiled and showed my appreciation. Then, it occurred to me, Do I get paid for this?

Barry: "By the way, what do I charge you, or is everything here free?"

Peter: "Nothing is free, Barry, especially in Heaven, so don't worry, you'll get paid, and thanks for the haircut. It's a real honor to be the first to get a haircut from you here. I wish you luck in your new shop, and I know you'll find Heaven to be everything you hoped it would be."

He paused for a second and then added, "And I'm truly sorry about your dream."

As he started to walk out, I wondered about one thing.

Barry: "Hey, Peter, if it was up to you, would you

have let me into Heaven?"

Peter: "I don't know. I never did any research on you. You had a VIP pass. I have never seen one of those before. All I can say is, He must have wanted you pretty bad."

Chapter III

While I was waiting for The Big Kahuna to appear, I started watching the baseball game. It was the ninth inning, and the Dodgers were at-bat with two outs, a run behind, with a runner on first. Enrique Castro was at the plate and the count was three and two. The next pitch was low, outside, and almost in the dirt. Castro swung the bat like it was a nine-iron, the ball sailed over the right-field fence and the game was over. As Castro crossed home plate, he hit his chest twice and pointed up, thanking God for the outcome.

Now yesterday, I would have thought nothing of it, but knowing what I know now, I couldn't help but laugh. It was the first time I had laughed since I got to Heaven, and I had to admit, it felt good. But this joke was nothing new. I had always found it funny that people were so self-centered; they thought God was watching over their every move. Now, there might be an outside chance that God is a baseball fan, but if that is true, I doubt He would find it much fun if He was always controlling the outcome.

It occurred to me that maybe I shouldn't be thinking like that. After all, who was I to think I understood God, and Peter did warn me that He could change on a dime. If my arrogance pissed Him off, He might remove His name from the window and I could spend eternity sitting on my ass on one of these big, comfy mid-century barber chairs with no customers.

Just then, the door opened, and in walked a tall, athletic, handsome young man. I thought to myself, could this be God?

He smiled and asked me, "Do you know how to do a fade?"

To play it safe, I figured I better give him my most honest answer: "I can do one, but I haven't done that many, so it takes me a little longer than others." Then I asked him if he was God?

He laughed and said no, but that he'd still give me a shot at cutting his hair.

Knowing he wasn't God, I told him I was sorry,

but I didn't have time right then, because God was on his way.

But the young man quickly responded not to worry. He had just come from God and He would be delayed. God stuff, I guess. With that, he sat down in the chair, and I said under my breath, "Ah, what the hell," and put the chair cloth around him and asked his name.

"Luc, and you must be Barry?" he replied.

I nodded yes. Being a curious person, I would always ask questions as I cut hair. Over the years, I had learned that although some of my clients would become annoyed at all my questions, most of them felt cheated if I didn't ask them. So, I started with the most obvious one.

Barry: "You're a tall guy – ever play basketball?"

Luc: "No, I'm not much into sports. I'm more into the arts."

Barry: "So, what kind of artist are you – a painter, sculptor, musician, actor…author?"

Luc: "No, I'm more like a muse. I inspire artists."

Barry: "What a cool thing to do. Have you inspired anyone I might have heard of?"

Luc: "Shakespeare, Mozart, Michelangelo, the Rolling Stones, Van Gogh, Kerouac. Pretty much all the great artists in history."

Barry: "Wow, what a great job! So, who was

your favorite?"

Luc: "Believe it or not, I would say Robert Johnson. I've always had a soft spot in my heart for the blues."

Having been a musician myself in my younger years, I remembered the legend of Robert Johnson, the devil, and the crossroads.

Barry: "Is it true that Robert Johnson went to a Mississippi crossroads and sold his soul to the devil to become a great blues guitar player?"

Luc chuckled.

Luc: "Well, I met him at a crossroads, and I think I inspired him to become a great blues guitarist, but he never sold me his soul."

Barry: "Wait! I don't understand. He never sold you his soul?"

Luc: "Yeah…I'm Lucifer. My friends call me Luc. You can call me Luc too if you like."

Barry: "You mean…you're the devil?"

He chuckled again.

Luc: "You could say that, but you better show me some sympathy, or I'll lay your soul to waste."

He broke out laughing. I didn't know if I should laugh or run out of the room. But before I could decide, he stopped laughing, stared deep into my eyes for what seemed like an eternity… then broke out laughing even louder.

Luc: "Relax, no one's gonna lay your soul to waste. Certainly not me and certainly not before you cut my hair. And even if I wanted to – which I don't – I couldn't. I'm just a simple archangel. I'm not God."

Barry: "But you're the devil, Satan, the Prince of Darkness."

Luc: "Being the Prince of Darkness is kinda like being the lead singer in a Bruce Springsteen cover band. Everyone says...he sounds just like Bruce, but everyone knows there's only one Bruce."

He paused for a moment and continued, "And there's only one God and quite frankly, He can keep the job. Do you have any idea what it's like to be God? Billions of people all over the universe asking for something twenty-four-seven and kvetching that they've been forsaken when they don't get it. Why would anyone want that job? I know I don't."

Barry: "Well, what about all that evil you caused?"

Luc laughed even harder: "The evil I caused? Talk 'bout the pot calling the kettle black. You'll have to tell that to God when you meet Him. He loves to laugh and that should make Him laugh out loud. Man just loves to blame anyone but himself for the messes he gets himself into. I had nothing to do with any of that stuff they blame me for. That's just bible crap. They needed a boogieman and looked no further than this fallen angel. I'm a muse. I don't control or punish people; I inspire them. It's man himself who can't seem to get out of his own way."

I remembered that was what Peter said and maybe it was true, but that raised another question.

Barry: "Well then, how did you get in so much trouble with God that He threw you out of Heaven?"

Luc: "Oh, you heard about that? Well, God has this obsession with free will. He gave it to man, and He gave it to us angels, but when I tried to use mine by telling him a joke about His monstrosity called Earth, He got pissed off and threw me out of Heaven. Granted, it probably wasn't my best joke, but after all, I was still new to the whole free will thing. I thought He'd think it was funny... Whoops!"

Barry: "But you're here now. Why did he let you back in?"

Luc: "Honestly, He missed me. After I was banished from Heaven, there was no one left that made Him laugh, and He really does love to laugh. Without me around, He became pissed off all the time. He turned into a God of wrath, spreading pestilence, and His heart was filled with vengeance. One day, He looked in the mirror and didn't like what he saw, so He summoned me back to Heaven. I think the deciding factor was when He found out that it was me that inspired the eight beatitudes, and it was His way of thanking me. See, Jesus and I were chilin' on the beach along the Sea of Galilee. When he realized how many people were there to hear him speak, Jesus got a little stage fright and had a panic attack. He was going to call the whole thing off, so I put on my muse cap and suggested the whole "Blessed are" speech. That seemed to calm him down, and the rest you know."

Barry: "What about Hell? Does it even exist?"

Luc: "Simply said, no, that was just more Bible stuff. They figured man would straighten up and fly right if he feared eternal fire and brimstone. Didn't work, though. The problem was, they also told man he could be forgiven by simply asking God. That part of their scripture opened Pandora's box. Man, like anyone with free will would prefer having fun over the boring act of being righteous. And why should they be righteous when all they had to do was sing His praises, ask for forgiveness, go to church on Sunday, and all is forgiven? Trust me, God is fair and forgiving, but He isn't naive. That's not to say that if you steal a candy bar when you're a kid, or break some silly human law, you won't get into Heaven, but He has a simple code to get in here. If your good outweighs your bad, you'll get in, and thank God it's that way. This place would be a ghost town if there wasn't that balance, and God knows it.

I guess you can't blame the disciples for that. They were all just trying to keep the flock together and pulled out every trick they could think of. Forgiveness being just one. Since they didn't really know what God expected from His children, they were just throwing spaghetti against the ceiling, hoping some of it would stick. I tried to tell them it didn't work that way, but who was going to listen to an archangel who had been thrown out of Heaven over a joke?"

Barry: "So what really happens to those that don't fly right?"

Luc: "Ashes to ashes, funk to funky. Some of the best song lyrics I ever inspired. What happens to those that don't fly right? They just disappear, shipped off to the edge of the Universe to the Nothing. No pain, no fire, just gone. After all, doesn't God have enough to do? I mean, ask yourself, if He created all this, why would He throw a wrench in the gears by allowing a Hell and an adversary to exist that would constantly be challenging His authority? He hasn't the time or the inclination for that kind of stupidness. He is all-powerful and being such, could destroy anyone or anything that challenges Him. When I pissed Him off, He could have easily cast me into that black hole, where I would cease to exist, but He wanted me to learn from my mistake and punished me much like a parent punishes their child. I guess you could say, He gave me a timeout."

I could have asked him a thousand more questions, but I needed to start concentrating on finishing his haircut. Looking at my work, I had to say, it might have been the best fade I had ever done. I didn't know if it was because I was scared to death of Luc, or because I felt I had to live up to being God's favorite barber, but it looked great!

Barry: "Is this what you were looking for?"

He looked into the mirror, smiled, and raised two thumbs in the air. My heart dropped to my knees, but I acted like that was the reaction I expected. Wanting to get rid of him as fast as I could, I made the final touches on his haircut and removed the cloth.

As he was walking out, he looked back in the mirror, one more time, and with a smile on his face said, "See, I knew you could do it. You just needed a little inspiration." Chuckling, he continued, "Even if it came in the form of utter fear."

I thanked him and took a deep sigh of relief. Although everything he said made sense, there was still that lingering thought that he was the "Prince of Darkness" or at best, a seraph. Either way, I was sure any disagreement between an archangel and a mortal man could only come to one conclusion, and that wouldn't be good for me. So, I thanked him for coming in and told him I hoped he would return.

As he opened the door to leave, he was knocked back by a very aggressive woman.

Luc: "Whoa, Gerty, where's the fire?"

The woman never even glanced in his direction and continued to move right toward me. I cautiously backed up a few steps, preparing for the pending impact when she stopped and sat down in the chair, leaned forward with her forearms on her knees, stared at me, and said, "What can you do with this head of hair?"

After a quiet sigh of relief, I began to explain to her that I was waiting for God, but it was as if she never heard a word I said. She just continued to stare at me. Or, should I say, through me. Before I could repeat that I was waiting for God, she asked, "You do cut women's hair, don't you?"

Barry: "As a rule, no, but since you wear your hair short, I think I could do it, but…."

Just then, Luc broke out in laughter and said, "Barry, let me introduce you to Gertrude Stein. Understand the word 'but' does not exist in her vocabulary."

Gertrude looked over in Luc's direction and remarked, "Why, Luc, how are you? Have you been there long?"

Luc: "Not long, Gerty. In fact, I was just leaving.

Allow me to introduce you to Barry. Barry is God's favorite barber, so I'm sure he will do a fine job on your hair."

Gerty: "I'm sure he will, as long as he hasn't been influenced by the likes of you. If such is the case, I may leave this establishment with regret."

Luc: "You will find no need for regret. Barry is a great barber and a curious man who relishes the question more than the answer. A trait not wasted on you, since you have all the answers."

Chapter IV

It was obvious that Gerty and Luc were not friends, but their conflict appeared more like a game of tennis than a prizefight. I thought to myself, The last thing I need is to get caught between the Prince of Darkness and the Queen of Intransigence, so I quickly asked her how she would like her hair cut.

Gertrude: "With purposefulness!"

With Purposefulness? What the hell does that mean? I glanced over at Luc with a confused look. He just laughed as he walked out of the room, holding his hand up to wave goodbye. A few seconds later from outside, I heard him yell, "HAVE FUN, BARRY."

I pretended I didn't hear him and turned my focus on her haircut. She sat there staring forward with a look of defiant anticipation.

Barry: "So, was your last haircut purposeful?"

Gerty: "It was good, but I would like it a bit shorter on top. My time is too valuable and my days too busy to be dealing with my hair."

With that, the room became as quiet as a church. To me, there was nothing worse than cutting hair in silence, so I began to make conversation.

Barry: "I've heard your name, but I admit, I have no idea who you are."

Gerty: "You must be kidding? Everyone knows who I am. Everyone important, that is."

Barry: "Well, I'm not very important, so I guess that explains it."

Gerty: "The sign in the window says you're God's favorite barber, that's pretty important."

Barry: "I guess, but I'm still just a barber. What did you do that made you so famous?"

Gerty: "There's nothing past tense about what I do. I'm a writer, a poet, a playwright, and a collector of fine art, but my greatest gift is helping other artists."

That explained the friction between her and Luc, but since he was gone and she was here, she got my undivided attention.

Barry: "So, have you ever collected art from any famous artist?"

Gerty: "Of course! Why would I collect art that has no value?"

I learned over the years that the best way to treat an antagonist was to ignore their attempts at confrontation.

Barry: "So, who are some of the artists in your collection?"

Gertrude: "Picasso, Matisse, Cézanne, Renoir and even a couple Toulouse-Lautrec."

Barry: "Wow! Did you ever meet any of them?"

Gerty: "Many times. Picasso even painted my portrait, although many said it didn't look like me. They all used to come to my flat in Paris on Saturday nights. We would discuss their work. Most artists desperately require encouragement, and I provided it with honest integrity. All except Dali. All that little shit needed was a large nail in the side of his inflated ego. Anyway, together we created what is now called the Modernist period. I also had many writers of the time in my salon. Fitzgerald, Wilder, Thornton, and my student and the biggest disappointment of my life, Hemingway. He considered me his mentor and would never send in a manuscript before showing it to me. Sadly, he couldn't take a joke. I called him yellow in my book, The Biography of Alice B. Toklas. Since no one ever had the guts to call him yellow, I decided I would do it just to get a rise out of him. After it was published, he never spoke to me again."

This conversation was beginning to get interesting.

Barry: "So, is Alice B. Toklas a pen name of yours?"

Gerty: "Have you ever read a book or even gone into a library? Alice B. Toklas was my life partner."

Now it was coming back to me. I remembered reading somewhere that Stein was infamous for her lesbianism, but then, what was she doing in Heaven? The Bible seemed pretty clear that homosexuality was a sin. What an odd place this Heaven was. Nothing about it made sense. I could wait until I spoke to God, but my inquisitiveness might only make Him angry, so I decided I would ask her first.

Barry: "I'm just a simple barber and am easily confused, but what are you doing in Heaven? I thought homosexuality was a sin. I don't have a problem with it myself, but they sure seem to have one in the Bible."

She began to laugh from the deepest part of her belly and could barely get her words out through her laughter.

Gerty: "The Bible? Oh please, there's no there, there. Most of the New Testament was written forty years after Jesus died by followers of his followers. Who has that kind of memory? Plus, fourteen books were removed sixteen hundred years after his death. And if you read the four gospels, there's one contradiction after another. The Bible…come on. If Hemingway had brought that poor excuse for literature to me, I would have used it for kindling. But don't believe me, ask God Himself. You have met Him, haven't you?"

Barry: "No."

Gerty: "Well, when you do, ask Him what He thinks about the Bible. He always enjoys a good laugh. Besides, even if the Bible was the Word of God, it said man should not lie with another man. It said nothing about a man loving another man. There is a big difference between sex and love. God is all about love and He doesn't care whom we love, as long as we love. Be it man with woman, man with man, or woman with woman. Many people, like Hemingway, never recognize that nuance. Of course, he never loved anyone except himself."

Barry: "Is he here in Heaven?"

Gerty: "Oh, hell no, and he would be glad to not be. As Clemens said, 'You go to Heaven for the weather, to Hell for the company.' I would suspect Earnest is much happier there."

Barry: "But I thought Hell didn't exist."

Gerty: "It doesn't, but no one could tell Hemingway."

With a chuckle, she continued, "He thought he was already in hell when he was living on Earth. Anyway, Alice and I had been in a loving, giving relationship for almost forty years on Earth until I died of cancer. Now we are here together again, and it continues to be a devoted romance like very few in human history. That's all God cares about. Not whether it's a man or woman. He has told me several times that making man and woman was one of His biggest mistakes. He could have accomplished what He wanted with much better results if He had stuck to just men. Of course, I think it would have been even better if it was just women."

Barry: "You mean God admits to making mistakes?"

Gerty: "Oh Heavens, no, but if you read between the lines, you know, He knows He got that one wrong."

By now I had completely stopped cutting her hair and was sitting on the stool I used when doing the final touches.

Barry: "You mentioned Twain. He's my favorite author. Is he here in Heaven?"

Gerty: "Oh yeah, he's here and he deserves to be. He has more integrity in his pinky finger than most men will ever have in their whole bodies. I didn't know him on Earth, but we've become good friends here. He's a very witty man with a sharp tongue and a flair for exposing the obvious. He's God's favorite writer. Just like you are God's favorite barber. By the way, how about getting back to cutting my hair?"

I felt embarrassed and went back to the finishing touches on her hair, but I wanted to ask her one last thing.

Barry: "Do you have any idea why God picked me to be His favorite barber?"

Gerty: "Well, so far, it's a good haircut, but I've had good haircuts before. It must be you, not your barbering skills. Don't get me wrong, you are talented and I can say I've never had a better haircut, but I've had haircuts just as good. You tell me, why do you think He picked you?"

Barry: "I wish I knew. I was all set to jump onto my sailboat and write my memoirs when I wound up here. I'm a good guy, but certainly not a great person. I have a whole lot of flaws and if I were God, I would never pick me."

Gerty: "You're a writer?"

Barry: "Well, I wouldn't go that far, but I do enjoy putting words on paper."

Gerty: "Do you have anything here I could read?"

I was about to say no when I saw a notebook on the table titled If Hair Could Talk. I had always thought that would be a good title for my memoirs, but I had never written it down. I guess God can read minds. Acting like I knew it had been there all along, I said, "Yeah" and grabbed the notebook and opened it. Inside, there were about twenty pages I had written about a week ago and never proofread, but I figured what the hell and handed it to her.

Gerty blazed through it at incredible speed. When she had read it all, she put it down and seemed to savor the moment like a cup of hot tea, looking up and rubbing her neck like she seemed to be trying to find the right words.

Gerty: "There's talent there. It's a bit primitive, but with a little practice and my help, we just might make an author out of you."

Wait! Did I hear right? Did Gertrude Stein, the muse for some of the greatest authors of the twentieth century, just say I had talent? How do I respond to that? Should I act like that's what I expected, or should I seem excited? No matter what my response would be, if I was to be an author, I better find the right words to express my gratitude.

Barry: "Really? Thanks!

Really? Thanks? That was the best I could do?

Gerty: "I'll tell you what. You write twenty more pages before my next haircut, and if they are as good as these twenty pages, I will sit down with you and we can go over all of it. Are we done here?"

I was in shock and couldn't get the words out of my mouth, so I just nodded. She got up, walked to the door, and opened it, but before she walked out, she turned around.

Gerty: "Don't force it. If it doesn't come one day, it will come another day. As you write more, it will get easier. Most importantly, keep it honest. Readers will see right through anything that isn't."

She looked at herself one last time in the mirror and said, "Nice haircut. I will send Van Gogh over to get his haircut."

With that, she left with the same forthrightness she had entered with, but as she walked out, without looking back, she said with her usual forceful voice, "Remember, keep… it… honest!"

After she left, I cleaned up and sat down in the barber chair. I must have been staring out the window for several minutes, just soaking in what she had said. There's talent there. Talent, I had talent. Who knew? I began to run through the gumbo of stories and thoughts in my head, trying to sort them out, but I was confused by her last comment: Keep it honest. What the hell did that mean? I only knew one way to write. How would I know if I was being honest?

Over the years, I had been told by many of my friends, family, and clients that I had a habit of losing myself in my thoughts. I could go so deep into them that I would lose all connection with my surroundings. I must have been in one of those moments because I never heard the door open or the man walk in. What I did hear was a voice from behind me saying sarcastically, "So, you're God's favorite barber."

Without looking back, I responded, "Yep, that's what the sign says." Then it occurred to me that maybe this was God. I better play it safe and show some respect. So, I turned quickly to apologize, "I'm sorry, can I help you?"

Standing in front of me was a lean man in his fifties. His hair was a bit overgrown and sticking out on one side. He looked at me with the same sarcasm on his face as he had spoken with. I realized this wasn't just anyone. I knew this guy. I knew him as well as I knew myself. My mind said it was impossible, but my eyes were looking right at him. Was this some cruel joke that Luc – I mean, Lucifer – was playing on me, or some kind of test from God?

What did it matter – it was him.

My eyes began to tear up a bit and with a stammer in my voice, I asked, "Dad? Is that you?"

Chapter V

He looked down at himself as if to make sure, smiled, and said, "Yep, it's me. How are you, son?"

For a moment, I didn't know quite what to do. The shock of seeing him had left me speechless and numb. The look on his face said he didn't know what to do either. I did the only thing I could think of. I walked over to him slowly, but with intent, and put my arms around him, hugging him like I would never let go. Like most men from his generation, my father was never an affectionate guy, but I didn't care. To my surprise, he hugged me too.

After savoring the moment, we both seemed to let go of the other at the same time, but I kept my hands on his arms as I asked, "How are you?'

Dad: "If I was any better, I'd have to be two people."

I must have heard him say that thousands of times in my life, but this time, it sounded like he really meant it. I don't remember ever seeing such a big smile on his face. I was savoring every second of this moment when it suddenly occurred to me.

Barry: "Mom's here, isn't she?"

Dad: "Of course. She was a sure thing to get into Heaven. She stayed home because she figured it would be better for you and me to spend a little time together first, but she's excited to see you."

That sounded like Mom. Always making the sacrifice for us. It was a hard job, being his wife and my mother since he and I agreed on very little, but it occurred to me that God might walk in on us at any time to get His haircut.

Barry: "Dad, we may have to end this soon. I think God is on His way."

Dad: "Oh, don't worry about Him. He sent me here. How 'bout cutting my hair?"

Now, in all the years I was a barber, I had only cut my dad's hair twice. Once in barber school and once right after I graduated. I think it was an unspoken agreement that it would be better for our relationship that way.

Barry: "Yeah, of course, I can cut your hair. If

you want me to."

Dad: "Well, you're God's favorite barber. Who wouldn't want God's favorite barber to cut his hair?"

He sat down. I wrapped him up and began to cut his hair. After a couple of minutes, I noticed the conversation had gone silent. Knowing my father wouldn't initiate it, I stepped up.

Barry: "So, what are you doing to keep busy?"

Dad: "I try to keep busy. Still doing my woodworking, making my stain glass lampshades, and I ride my bike a lot all over Heaven."

He paused as if considering whether to say the next thing.

Dad: "Oh yeah, Louie Tiffany actually asked if he could have one of my lampshades."

Barry: "You're kidding, that's so exciting! Sounds like you're happy here."

Dad: "I guess. What's happy?"

There you go, now that's my dad. It wasn't that he didn't know what happy was; he just didn't know how to be happy. He was never given the time to be happy in his life. Since he was a teenager, he had lived his life always being responsible for someone and never had time to himself. First, it was his mother and two kid brothers, then his mom was hit and killed by a car and at the age of seventeen, he was left to care for two boys with no family or friends to help. World War II broke out, and although he was still responsible for his kid brothers, he felt he had to go fight in the war. So, he made arrangements for his kid brothers, and off to war he went.

After the war, he married Mom, I was born, and he had the responsibilities of a husband and father. In later years, Mom got dementia and he took care of her, never complaining through his dying day. The truth was, there were moments when he was happy, but those were the moments when he was helping someone. I was hoping that it would be different here, that he had found real happiness for himself, but I guess the die had been cast.

Barry: "Well you look good, Dad."

Dad: "So do you, son. How are you enjoying your time in Heaven so far?"

Barry: "I guess it's okay. I've met some pretty interesting people so far, although I am disappointed that I couldn't live out my dream back on Earth."

Dad: "You mean that boat thing? That's all that was, a dream."

I thought, here we go again. It seemed that bursting my bubble was one of the few pleasures in his life. It got so bad at one point in our lives that we didn't speak for almost a year because he tried to force his old-fashioned values on me and I wouldn't have anything to do with them. Finally, my mother called and begged me to come to dinner. I told her I would, but if he said one thing negative about my lifestyle, I would walk out. I guess she read him the riot act because he never said a word. Eventually, he learned to respect my way of life, and in the last couple of years, we became close friends. But before we could make up for the decades of fighting, he died. I always felt cheated by his death, but now, here he was and I felt like I had been given a second chance.

So, I decided to ignore his comment, but before I could say anything, he continued.

Dad: "I'm not saying it wasn't a good idea, but for some reason inside, that voice in my head said it would never happen and you know how I used to tell you to listen to that voice in your head. Anyway, it's great to see you, Barry, and I want you to know how very proud I am of you."

I didn't quite know how to respond to that. He had never spoken to me with such pride. In fact, nothing I ever did seemed to be good enough for him.

Maybe that was for my benefit. Maybe that was his way to try to teach me to never be satisfied with anything less than perfection. After all, even if there was no such thing as perfection, every parent wanted their child to be perfect. I wanted to say all that, but all I could say was thanks.

For some reason, he looked down and saw my

notebook, picked it up, and began to read.

Dad: "Did you write this?"

Barry: "Yeah, it's just a thing I do for fun."

He continued to read for a couple more minutes and then looked up and said, "This is pretty darn good."

In his world, that meant really good. I struggled for words, but he beat me to it.

Dad: "I always knew you had it in you. You got this from your mom. I couldn't write a word if my life depended on it."

Of course, that was complete bullshit. His Master's thesis was still recommended reading, but that's what he did. He always gave Mom the credit for everything. It should be said, in the history of mankind, no man ever loved a woman more than he loved my mother. He never displayed anything but complete devotion to her. I never once heard them fight and God knows she could be stubborn as a mule. Whether she was right or wrong, he never broke from the character of a loving husband. Also, I would never have admitted it to him, but when he was alive, I envied his commitment to detail. After he was gone, I tried to commit myself to that philosophy and at this moment, I wanted him to know that.

Barry: "It wasn't all Mom. You taught me the joy of doing everything in my life to the best of my abilities, so take a bow and accept that you had a great influence on my life."

Dad: "Thanks, son, that means a lot. If that's true, could you try to do that side of my hair that always sticks out right this time?"

I laughed, but there was a part of me that thought he might be serious, so I focused all my efforts on that side of his head.

Dad: "So Mom wants to know if you can come over for dinner. She said she would make a meatloaf, and there's someone she wants you to meet."

Her meatloaf was my favorite, and I wondered who this person could be.

Barry: "I would, Dad, but I don't even know where I'm going to sleep tonight."

Dad: "Oh, nobody sleeps here. Everyone here is so busy doing what they love to do, that they never get tired. That doesn't mean we don't have free time, but time is a four-letter word up here."

Time is a four-letter word? That was my mantra. I began to think, was it just happenstance that these people had appeared for a haircut, or was this some sort of a plot orchestrated by God? I did have to admit though, so far, I was really enjoying Heaven. I had pretty much forgotten about my dream and couldn't wait to see who would be the next to sit in my chair. But there was one thing I wanted to do more than cut hair. That was to write.

Barry: "I just want to make sure I have time to write. I just cut Gertrude Stein's hair, and she thinks I have talent."

Dad: "If that crazy woman says you have talent, you can take it to the bank. And don't worry, there will be plenty of time for both. Just make sure you save a little time for Mom and me."

Barry: "Of course, but how will I find you? Maybe you should leave me an address and directions?"

Dad: "That's not necessary. Everyone you love and who loves you lives just around the corner. You'll recognize the house. It looks just like the one you grew up in."

There was no doubt, Heaven was an intriguing place. It seemed that everything I thought I knew had been thrown out the window and replaced with something better. I finished his haircut and all that was left was to blow it out, like he always did, and use a little hairspray to keep it in place. The side that always stuck out was lying in place perfectly. With great pride, I turned him toward the mirror to show him the results of my hard work.?"

Dad: "Perfect! I guess it only took you dying to get it right."

We laughed as I removed the chair cloth. It had been a long time since I heard him laugh, but what I heard next, I had never heard before.

Dad: "You've done good, son, and I don't mean just the hair."

There it was. The compliment I had waited my whole life to hear. But before I could say anything, he continued, "Now when you get a break, come by and see Mom. She's excited to see you and the meatloaf will be waiting."

For a moment, he just sat in the chair and I couldn't help but notice a bit of wetness in his eyes. He got up, walked over, put his arms around me, and hugged me like I would disappear if he let go. Despite that tear in his eye and a crack in his voice, there was a smile on his face.

Dad: "We love you, son, and we've missed you terribly. Don't be too long before you come by."

This might be the first time in my life he had let his guard down in front of me. Maybe the first time he ever let his guard down to anyone. I put my arms around him and kissed him on the cheek.

Barry: "I missed you guys so much, and I promise to come by as soon as I can. Tell Mom I love her."

As he walked out, I thought, could any day be more perfect? And although I had no idea when I could visit them, like everything else here so far, I was sure I would know when the time was right. I picked up the notebook and began to write, but I wasn't writing about those customers from my old shop; I was writing about my first day in Heaven. It flowed out of me like a plagiarist stealing a story, except it was my own story and my own words. Suddenly, I understood what Gerty meant. The words were honest. They came from deep inside and although I was still confused about all that was going on, my hand seemed to be able to make sense of it on paper. I couldn't put the pen down. As I wrote, all I could think about was who would be next in this amazing journey.

Chapter VI

It seemed like I had been writing for hours, but time, here in Heaven, was like playing football with no end zones. Of course, why wouldn't it be? After all, we were here forever. What a chilling thought. I found it hard to wrap my head around the fact that I would always be here, and as much as I dreaded dying when I was on Earth, I wasn't sure if eternity was any better.

But for now, I decided to shelve those thoughts and keep writing when the door opened and in came a man dressed to the nines, with a perfectly tailored suit, a very neatly folded pocket square, and a straw bowler hat.

Not wanting to ignore him for fear he might be

God, I said, respectfully, "Welcome, sir. How can I be of service to you?"

He smiled and said, "I'm in need of a trim. It's important to maintain my appearance, you know." He had a thick Italian accent that was almost comical.

I thought to myself, this couldn't be God, but after all that had happened so far, I wasn't going to take a chance, so I said, "Have a seat, sir."

With a sense of style and purpose, he hung his coat neatly on a hanger, put his hat on a hook, and sat down. His smile was contagious, and I found I couldn't help but smile too.

I put the chair cloth around him and said, "So, how is your day going?" My benign question only made him smile bigger like he knew exactly what I was doing.

"It's been a very productive day so far, and how's yours?" he replied.

I countered by saying, "It's been very enlightening."

He laughed as if he knew exactly what I meant. I asked him how he would like his hair cut. He told me he got his hair cut every week, but all he needed today was a cleanup around the ears and back, with a razor line along the neck. I hadn't done a haircut like that since barber school, but I remember being pretty good at them, so I got out my clippers and began cleaning up his neck. I still didn't know for sure if this was God, but there was only one way to find out

"My name is Barry, what's yours?" I asked.

He paused for a moment in thought, like he was looking for the right words, and said, "Oh, I know who you are. You're God's favorite barber. My name is Ponzi, Carlo Pietro Giovanni Guglielmo Tebaldo Ponzi, but please...call me Carlo"

I thought to myself, Carlo Ponzi, where do I know that name from? Then it hit me, Ponzi, the Ponzi scheme. This guy was a swindler. What in the world was he doing in Heaven? I remembered what Peter said about being surprised who was here, but this guy was a liar and a cheat and flimflammed people out of their money. I thought, Should I play dumb or curious about how he got here? And although it would be easier to play dumb, that had never been my style.

Barry: "I'm sorry, but maybe you could help me understand something. On Earth, you were a swindler, a liar, and a con man. One of the most famous con men of the twentieth century. You spent your life cheating people out of their money. How did you get into Heaven?"

My question brought an even bigger smile to his face that led to a chuckle.

Carlo: "You'll never hear me deny being a swindler.

In fact, I take pride in it. Even before I became a con man, I was a common thief, but I never stole from people who needed the money. I stole from a bank where I worked, got caught, and paid the price in jail. But while I was in jail, I got smart. I came up with a way to get people to willingly give me their money. Anyone with half a brain could have figured out that I was offering the impossible, but they not only gave me their money, they gave it to me with enthusiasm. All I had to do was play to their most dominant human trait: greed."

Barry: "But you broke at least two of the Commandments. Thou shall not lie, and thou shall not steal."

Carlo: "Oh, my friend, if everyone who broke a couple of the Commandments were left out of Heaven, this would be a ghost town. Let me ask you something."

Barry: "Sure, go ahead."

Carlo: "Did you ever work on Sunday?"

Barry: "I did when I first became a barber. I didn't want to, but I had to."

Carlo: "Did you always obey your parents no matter what?"

Barry: "Of course not, no kid does."

Carlo: "Have you ever lied?"

Barry: "I try not to, but yes, there were times if it

wasn't very important and made someone feel better about something."

Carlo: "And most important, have you ever had sex out of wedlock?"

Barry: "Well, I never got married..."

Carlo: "Then you broke at least four of them and you're "God's favorite barber." I'm only guilty of breaking two. I told people that they could become rich by investing their money in an impossible scheme and used their greed to close the deal."

Barry: "But you stole money from other people. That's so much worse."

Carlo: "Oh.... I didn't steal from people. They willingly gave me their money. Besides, I didn't know that God had prioritized the Commandments."

Barry: "So, you're saying God has no problem with you taking other people's money?"

Carlo: "Actually, He thought it was funny. If you are to believe those Commandments, my clients were as guilty as me. They never asked how or where I would get the money, just when they would get it. So, where did that money come from that I promised them? From others and the Tenth Commandment says, You shall not covet...anything that is your neighbor's. By the way, I think it's time you learn something everyone here already knows. Those tablets that God supposedly wrote and gave to Moses, those Ten Commandments... God didn't write them or give them to him."

Barry: "You know that for a fact?"

Carlo: "Yeah, He told me. But don't believe me, just think about it. They are 'commandments,' but God wanted man to use his free will. Why would He set down specific rules for man to follow? His plan was always to leave man to his own devices and never expected us to be perfect creatures. If you lived a reasonably good life, you got into Heaven, if you didn't, well... you know what happens."

Barry: "If it wasn't God, who was it?"

Carlo: "No one knows for sure, but I have a theory."

Barry: "And what's your theory?"

Carlo: "Who was the first to use his free will and got expelled from Heaven for doing it? Who knew God in an up-close and personal way, whose life was spent inspiring people, and who was there on Earth at the time? Most important, who has a great sense of humor and probably got a big laugh from it?"

Barry: "You mean Lucifer?"

Carlo: "Makes sense, doesn't it? They weren't rules, they were a warning. Break these rules while using your free will and you risk never getting into Heaven."

Barry: "Yeah, I guess it makes sense. It would be a good way to warn man that there is a price to pay for that free will God gave him. So, what about you? Now that you're here, what do you do to pass the day?"

Carlo: "I motivate people. A very important job, if I do say so myself. There is a giant puncture wound in the side of Heaven. A disease, so to speak, of pandemic proportions."

Barry: "Really, what's that?"

Carlo: "Apathy. Everyone is excited by the expectation of eternal life, but once we get here and realize what forever is, we lose all that enthusiasm. We are no longer driven by time to finish things, so we become bored and procrastinate, losing all our drive to accomplish them. As they say in my homeland, domani è il sapore del giorno.

Barry: "What does that mean?"

Carlo: "Tomorrow is the flavor of the day. Now a few people, like yourself, may never seem to run out of things to do, but most people here don't have a passion for anything. They try one thing and when they get bored with it, they try something else. After a while, they just give up trying to find something else and apathy creeps in."

Barry: "Well, how bad can it be? Apathy was everyone's favorite pastime on Earth. Wouldn't a swift kick in the butt get them going?"

Carlo: "It's different here. On Earth, there is an

end. If you don't know what to do with your life, you either die after living a miserable life or commit suicide to get away from it. Not great options granted, but here, there are no such options, because there's no death. If you can't get over it, it only gets worse. Eventually, the person falls into a comatose state. They just stand there with a blank stare on their face. They don't move, they don't respond to anything but they don't die. The plan is to get to them before they reach that point. That's where I come in. I have been blessed with charm. I can charm the white off of linguini, so God put me in charge of tackling this dreaded pandemic."

I thought to myself, this is exactly what I was thinking before he came in. I can't imagine being passionate about anything for all of eternity.

Barry: "So, how bad is it? I mean, are you able to help them all yourself, or are there others like you that do this motivation thing?"

Carlo: "Oh, there's no way I could do it by myself. I don't know how many people are here, but if one out of ten people in history made it here, that would be billions. No one person has the time to help all of them and at some point, almost all of them will need help. He has many working on this motivation thing. Porn stars are always good for a quick, short-term fix. No one can make one feel better for a short time than a porn star. For longer-term fixes, He uses politicians. They are always good at putting a shine on bullshit, but people usually figure them out eventually and go right back to being apathetic. So, when He needs a more permanent fix, He calls me."

Barry: "A shine on bullshit? So, what you're saying is that God has no problem lying? That doesn't seem very Heavenly."

Carlo: "Well, as you said, sometimes it's better to lie if it helps a person feel better. The best thing to do is not to lie to them, but to get them to lie to themselves like I did when I was on Earth. If you can get someone to lie to themself, after a while, the lie becomes the truth."

Barry: "The lie becomes the truth?"

Carlo: "Yeah, man would rather believe a lie than face the truth. Take his Bible. There are so many contradictions throughout it, but believers want to believe so bad, they lie to themselves that it all makes sense. I simply make them feel their lives are special to God (which they are) and tell them God has a plan for them, but I never tell them what it is. Their trust in the Almighty inspires them to go do something. When they get bored with that, I tell them, God has a new plan for them. If you say it with conviction, they will believe it. Truth be told, God does have a plan, so I'm not lying."

Barry: "Really? What's His plan?"

Carlo: "His plan is to not have zombies standing around in Heaven. In a perfect Heaven, He wants His children to have the free will to decide what to do, but when they lose their motivation to do anything, I come along and give them, as you put it, a kick in the butt."

He broke out laughing.

Carlo: "It's amazing what people will believe. When I was on Earth, I got people to believe I had some magic beans that would grow their money by fifty percent. No one in their right mind should have ever fallen for that, but my clients wanted to believe it so bad, they were willing to throw out all common sense to make that fast buck. Maybe I did lie to my clients on Earth a bit, but more importantly, they lied to themselves. And they continued to lie to themselves right up to the time I ran out of new clients and there was no more money to give them. Ah…if there had only been the internet back then. I might have been able to go on forever."

Barry: "But you do admit you lied, right?"

Carlo: "Okay, maybe I lied a little, but what did I lie about? Money! God doesn't care about money. In fact, He hates it. He created His children to be equal in every way and money only skews that. Besides, God originally believed His creation was perfect, but it only took one serpent to expose to Him that there's no such thing as perfection. Even when the creation is His. He had to learn to accept man's flaws and that included an occasional lie. It doesn't bother Him that much unless the lie physically hurts people or damages His precious Earth, and we all know money has been the greatest source of that kind of hurt throughout history. Many, if not most, people, on Earth, worship the dollars in their pocket more than they worship God Himself. That's why He got a big yuk at what I did."

Barry: "I'm sure it wasn't funny to those who lost everything because of your lies."

Carlo: "But they didn't lose everything. All they lost was money. If they lost their position in their social circle, then their social circle was just as guilty of worshipping that money god. If they lost their loved ones, they were never loved in the first place, their money was. And if they lost their self-esteem, then they truly never had much self-esteem, to begin with.

He paused for a moment and continued, "I'm guessing you were not a rich man. Did money ever affect your self-esteem?"

Barry: "No, I guess it didn't."

Carlo: "It says on your window that you're God's

favorite barber. Money can't buy that."

What he said made sense, but all this talk about losing something only reminded me that I had lost my dream and I began to feel my anger returning.

Barry: "It's true, I never cared that much about money, but God took something much more important from me. He took my dream."

Carlo: "But it was only a dream, wasn't it? It wasn't real. Life's not about dreams, it's about passions and your passion is to write. He didn't take that away from you. You certainly don't need a boat to do that."

My anger turned into confusion. How did he know that? How did he know about the boat and how much I love to write? I became suspicious. Did God send him here to make me feel better and clear His name?

Barry: "We just met; how did you know all that? I never mentioned my boat or how much I love to write."

Carlo: "Oh, I was talking to Peter and he told me about the boat and Gerty told me about the writing. But that doesn't matter. What matters is your passion is to write and I'm sure God has no plans to take it away from you. By the way, Gerty says you're a pretty good writer. I would love to read something when you're ready."

All his answers made sense, but there was still something about what he said that didn't ring right, and I wondered, was he telling me the truth, or was he just using his persuasive powers to make me feel better?

Barry: "How do I know you're telling me the truth? After all, you admitted that your history isn't exactly full of it. Or should I say, you have a history of being full of it?"

Carlo: "That's fair, but I'm not telling you anything you don't already know. I'm only confirming it."

He certainly was convincing, and I could see why those people gave him their money. Maybe he was right. Maybe the boat wasn't as important as I thought it was. Maybe it was the writing, and I had to admit the people I'd met here so far were far more interesting than my customers back on Earth. Maybe it was worth losing my boat dream for a better one. Besides, now I could write as much as I wanted and there were no day-to-day worries or time frames to contend with. I wanted to ask him more, but the haircut was pretty much over and so I said, "I guess I'm convinced!"

I turned him toward the mirror and used a hand mirror to show him the back, asking, "By the way, is this what you were looking for?"

Carlo: "Exactly what I was looking for, thank you."

I took the chair cloth off, gave him a good brushing, and he got up, put on his coat and hat with the same purpose and style, thanked me, and headed toward the door. As he opened the door, he looked one more time in the mirror, stood up a little straighter, smiled, and I was sure I heard him whisper something to himself that sounded like mission accomplished.

Barry: "I'm sorry, I couldn't hear you. What did you say?"

Carlo: "Nothing. Just admiring myself."

Chapter VII

As soon as Carlo left the room, I reached for my notebook and began writing. Gerty was right. The more I wrote, the easier it got, but when it came time to read what I wrote, all I could think about was who would be the next person to walk through my door. I just sat there for a few minutes, watching people walk by my window, but no one looked familiar and no one was coming in to get their haircut. That was okay. I had been blessed with the gift of patience and there was no doubt in my mind that sooner than later, one of them would come in.

I always loved looking out of the window in my shop on Earth. I felt the window in that shop was like a portal into the souls of the people passing by. Unlike Earth, the people walking by here all had smiles on their faces and everyone would greet those passing the other way. On an occasion, one would even look through the window and wave to me. No one seemed to be in a hurry. Of course, that probably had something to do with time being nonexistent here. It felt good to just sit there and watch them go by. It was the first time since I got here that I'd had the time to relax and appreciate my new digs.

After sitting there in the shop alone for a while, I began to wonder if I was destined to live, by myself, in this shop for eternity. When I was on Earth, I always had girlfriends. I never found that someone special, but mortality might have had something to do with that. I lived by that infamous axiom, "So many women, so little time," but now, I was looking straight into the face of eternity. Maybe it was time to set new standards and seek out that special someone? But was my perfect woman, my soul mate, out there somewhere in Heaven? And with billions of people in Heaven, what were the chances I would ever find her?

I admit I felt a certain amount of envy toward my parents and Gerty. They had found the perfect love story before they got here. Although the truth is, I was never interested in looking for that perfect love story. More than likely, I was just afraid to dive into the deep end of that love pool.

Fear, what an interesting concept. Like love, it can move mountains. Not only is it the opposite of love, but you could make the argument that fear, not love, is man's most prevalent emotion. So, how does someone fight fear? A better question is why did God create fear in the first place? I had returned to that place where my mind had taken over my consciousness when a voice interrupted my thoughts:

"Got time for a haircut?"

This time I turned quickly and there was a guy with thick shoulder-length hair and a well-overgrown dark beard. All you could see through the hair and beard was a pair of dark round sunglasses and a thin pointy nose. I quickly said, "Sure." After all, even if this wasn't God, I didn't know when He would arrive. I could deal with that if and when it happened, so I motioned for him to have a seat. He sat down and I put the cloth around him. "How would you like your hair cut?"

He said, "I haven't had a haircut since I arrived in Heaven, so please cut it way back. But before you cut the hair, do me a favor and cut off the beard? It's driving me crazy."

His voice was soft but clear with a thick Scouse accent and a tone of sadness. Now usually, I would cut the hair first, but I thought, what the hell. I picked up my clipper, pulled his hair out of the way, and started to cut off the beard.

Shaving beards was like mining for gold. You never knew what you would find underneath it, but the more I cut, the more I realized I had hit the motherlode.

Barry: "You're John Lennon, aren't you?"

John: "Yeah, but don't tell anyone."

Over the years, I had cut the hair of a lot of celebrities and my success with them was that I never treated them any different than I would the local plumber. In most cases, they appreciated it, but this was John Lennon, my favorite member of my favorite band. Still, I knew I couldn't act star-struck, so, kiddingly I said, "Why, are you hiding from someone?"

John: "Yeah, from everyone."

He sounded serious, so I just went back to cutting his beard. He wasn't at all like I imagined him. Very quiet. I think we went about five minutes without a word being spoken. A rare moment for me. I decided to just keep cutting. I was staring at his hair so I wouldn't stare at him, but in my head, I kept repeating to myself, It's John Lennon, John Frickin' Lennon.

Just then I heard the door open behind me and a voice started singing, "I'm so tired, I haven't slept a wink."

John motioned for me to stop and sat up, looked back behind me, and began to sing, "I wonder should I call you, but I know what you would doooo." Then the two of them began to sing the chorus in harmony. John jumped out of the chair, went over to the guy, and with the first smile I had seen on his face, gave the other guy a giant hug. It seemed like a giant weight had been lifted off of his shoulders. The two started laughing and kept hugging.

John: "Where the hell have you been?"

The other guy laughed and said, "Around here, there, and everywhere. I was walking by and saw you sitting in the chair."

John: "Well, have a seat, and let's catch up."

The other guy sat down in the other mid-century barber chair. I turned John's chair in that direction while still staring at his hair so I wouldn't seem like a groupie, but I noticed he still had a smile from cheek to cheek.

John: "Where are my manners? My auntie would have my guts for garters. This is my new barber, Barry. Barry, this is my bandmate and good friend, George."

Could this be happening? Did I just get a private Beatles concert? John and George singing together. Now I knew for sure I was in Heaven.

Barry: "It's a great pleasure to meet you. To meet both of you."

I decided that was enough and just let the two of them reunite.

George: "Have you seen Brian?

John: "Yeah, and Harry too."

George: "Well, it shouldn't be much longer, and we can get the band back together."

John: "That's what Brian said, but I told him I wasn't interested."

George: "You're not still mad at Paul, are you?"

John: "No. I just don't want to go through all that again. Enough is enough. Besides, I hated my character in the group. Paul was the cutie, you were the mysterious one, Ringo was the adorable one, and I was the class clown. Never again."

George: "What are you talking about? Paul might have been the cutie when he was young, but have you seen him lately? And I was as mysterious as a book of matches in a bathroom. Ringo may be adorable and I love him, but he will always be the fool on the hill."

They both let out a big laugh.

George: "You weren't the class clown; you were the leader of the group. We'd have been nothing without you."

John: "I don't know if that's true. I always felt

like the disposable one."

He looked over his shoulder at me

John: "Hey, Barry, who was your favorite Beatle?"

I was lost for words. What a question to ask one of their biggest fans, but I tried to stay neutral.

Barry: "I don't have a favorite Beatle, just favorite Beatle songs and don't ask what they are, because they change all the time."

George laughed and looked at John.

George: "If he's as good a barber as he is a diplomat, this will be the best haircut you've ever gotten."

His comment made me laugh out loud.

Barry: "You know...Diplomacy is a required course in barber school."

George: "Well you must have received an A+."

With that, George looked over at John and stood up,

George: "I gotta run, Johnny. I'm meeting up with Ravi. I just wanted to come in and say hello. One day very soon, I'll come and fetch you back to my home and we'll have lunch, go for a long walk in my garden, and catch up."

John: "I'd love that, mate. And don't forget, when you need a haircut, you know where to come."

He pointed to the window and smiled.

John: "After all, Barry is God's favorite barber."

George: "Can't ask for any more than that, can you? I'll see you soon, Johnny, and Barry, I'll see you soon too. It's been a pleasure to meet you."

Barry: "Believe me, the pleasure was all mine. And thanks for the mini-concert."

They both laughed as George got up to leave. John sat back in his chair, but he was a different person. For the first time since he had come in, he looked like the John Lennon I imagined.

John: "I can't tell you how much I needed that. Brian is like a father, and Harry is a guilty pleasure, but George… George is my brother.

Barry: "So why didn't you search him out?"

John: "Good question and one I have no good answer for. I guess I was afraid."

Barry: "Afraid of what?"

John: "Another good question I have no answer for. Fear doesn't always have a good reason. I'm just glad I came in to get my hair cut and that George saw me in the window.

I thought maybe this was divine intervention rather than coincidence, but I wasn't sure, so I kept it to myself. It didn't matter. All that mattered was that he seemed much happier than when he came in and I felt I had gained his trust.

Chapter VIII

Barry: "So, have you spoken to God since you've been here?"

John: "A couple of times."

Barry: "Did you ask Him why He took you at such a young age? I've always been curious why the good die young."

John: "He said the original plan was for me to survive. He thought I could serve Him as a prophet and the shooting would put me back on the front page, inspiring people to follow my message of love."

Barry: "So, why did He change His mind?"

John: "He decided I was too snarky and eventually, no one would take me seriously. But to be completely honest, He didn't change His mind; I changed it."

Barry: "You changed it, why?"

John: "I'd done everything I set out to do, and everything I was doing at that point was nothing more than a bad caricature of who I was. I found myself doing what the fans wanted, not what I wanted, and was tired of always being afraid there was someone that might be coming up from behind to knock my legs out from under me. Turned out I was right although Chapman did me and the world a favor. For just a moment in time, there was love all around the world. Fearless, unconditional love, which was all I ever wanted. That, and for people to love me for who I was, not what I was. Who could ask for more than that at the end of their life?"

Barry: "Yoko loved you for who you were, didn't she?"

John: "Yeah, and she still does, but I was afraid of her love and demanded too much from it. I acted like I wanted to be left alone, but I was really afraid of being alone like I was as a kid. My fear that she would stop loving me and I'd wind up back in that place was just too much. The only time I ever felt true, fearless love in my life, was when I was with Sean, but the world wouldn't let me be in that place. They wanted more and more from Beatle John."

I went back to cutting his hair thinking, There

it is. Love and fear in a battle for supremacy. What was God thinking? The room went quiet again. I hate when that happens, so I asked him another question.

Barry: "I know this is off the wall, but do you have any idea why God put fear in man's heart? I was thinking about that before you came in. I understand love, but I don't understand fear. Especially since most fear is usually nothing more than ghosts in the closet. We think there is something to be afraid of, but most of the time, it's just our own shadow."

John: "That's a great question. You should ask Him when you meet him."

I laughed and said, "I'm afraid to ask Him."

John smiled. "Don't be. He's pretty much an open book if you sincerely want to know. I once asked why I was here after the things I said in 'Imagine.' He said because I said imagine. I didn't say there was no Heaven, but rather 'Imagine there's no Heaven' and He understood what I was saying."

He paused in thought. "I agree with you; the world would be better off without fear. Imagine how nice it would be if we didn't need to fear God to live a virtuous life? Could you imagine what the world would be like if all love was fearless? It would free our minds and open our hearts. You may have just inspired me to write another verse for 'Imagine.'"

Laughing, I said, "Maybe I should change the sign on my window to Barber and Muse. I can't say I disagree with you about fear, and it's certainly not my place to say anything, but if you believe that, why didn't you live a more virtuous life?"

John: "It was safe hiding behind my wisecracks and antics. As you said, fear is powerful and the most uncontrollable emotion of all. I guess I was trying to hide from my own shadow. Being snarky was just a defense mechanism. A wall to hide behind. Even Yoko's love wasn't enough for me to come out from behind the wall. It took Sean. That was unconditional and fearless love. No conditions and no fear, from either of us, just pure love. So Barry, is there someone special you left back on Earth?"

Barry: "Not really. I was always hoping she would appear out of the blue, but she never did. Truth be told, I was afraid just like you. Not afraid of love, but afraid to love. I was afraid of the pain I might feel if she didn't feel the same or, along the way, lost it."

John: "So, you and I aren't that different."

I laughed and said, "I think we are very different, Mr. Lennon."

John: "Please, call me John."

Barry: "Okay, John."

His name kinda got caught in my throat as I said it. I thought how cool it was to be on a first-name basis with my favorite Beatle. My favorite Beatle? Wait, that's exactly what he hated being. Now I was guilty of what he hated most.

As I trimmed the hair around his ears, there was one question I couldn't get out of my head. Why did God create love and then push back at it by creating fear? It made no sense, but then I thought, When you think about it, neither does love. It occurred to me, what did someone who spent his life writing songs about love think of love now that he was here in Heaven?

Barry: "Do you still believe love is all we need?"

John: "I have to admit, I'm not as sure as I used to be and after this conversation, I'm doubting it even more. With few exceptions, love has brought man so much pain and heartache. Almost every crime in man's history has been a result of man's inflated interpretation of love. The love of money, the love of a woman, the love of fame and glory, and the love of power.

Barry: "Are you saying love is bad?"

John paused again, to think for a moment while I kept cutting.

John: "I have always seen love as the light and never looked at its shadow. Inside that shadow is its selfishness. People always say I love my girl, my dog, my child, my work, my, my, my. God's love was never intended to be a possession for self-gratification. By the way, your curiosity makes you an easy person to talk to."

Barry: "That might be the most important class at barber school. They call it Communication 101 and it always starts with a question."

John laughed and said, "Well, you must have gotten straight A's in barber school."

Barry: "The truth is, I'm only as good as the person I'm questioning."

I thought, Enough of this mutual admiration crap. I wanted to know more about him, without seeming like a fan.

Barry: "So, have you written any songs since you got here?"

John: "No music, but I still love to draw. Wait, there's that word again."

Barry: "I was thinking about that. I've been writing my memoirs and 'loving' every minute."

John: "So, you're an author? I knew you were more than just a good barber."

Barry: "Calling me an author is a bit of a stretch. I'm writing a memoir of my experiences behind the chair, but I do admit, writing is like really good sex – I can't get enough."

John: "Trust me, you can get enough of really good sex. I sure did. That's why I fell in love with Yoko. Not that the sex wasn't good, but she was so much more than just good sex and if you're honest, you would say your writing is too. In fact, if it isn't, you're wasting your time."

Barry: "Good point, John. I guess it's fearless love. I don't care what other people think of it, but I can't imagine not writing. By the way, I'm very curious about something. Did God send you here?

John: "No, I just saw the sign and thought I'd give you a try. Why do you ask?"

Barry: "Because I'm pretty sure that every other haircut I've given since I got here was someone sent by God. I'm beginning to think He has some grand plan for me, but I can't figure out what it could be."

John: "As far as I know, I'm not part of any grand plan, although I'm glad I came in for a haircut. I haven't talked to anyone since I got here and I've so enjoyed our conversation. Thank you, Barry, thanks a lot. Now, let's see if you are as good a barber as you are a therapist."

He smiled the biggest smile of the day as I turned him toward the mirror.

John: "Looks like I got a twofer. The haircut is exactly what I was looking for. The only problem is, when I walk home, everyone will know who I am.

The funny thing is, I don't care anymore. The light is on and the shadows are gone. Who knows, maybe I'll go home and write a new song. Thanks again, Barry, and you will be getting a lot of referrals from me."

Barry: "Thank you! But don't send me too many or I might not have the time to write. I love cutting hair and meeting interesting people like yourself, but writing is my true passion and I don't want barbering to take time away from it."

John: "You got it, but isn't your writing based on the people you meet here and the more you meet, the more you write?"

Just then, the door opened like it was on cue and there was Peter.

Peter: "Hey, John, how are you? Boy, do you look a whole lot better."

John: "I am, in more ways than you know, Peter, and I owe it all to Barry."

Peter: "Yeah, he's pretty darn good, isn't he?"

John: "You'll never know how good."

Peter: "Oh, I think I do. Barry, God asked me to stop by and tell you to take a break and go see your parents. They're waiting for you. I hear there's a slice of meatloaf waiting with your name on it.

There seemed to be no secrets here in Heaven, but I didn't care right then. I was just happy to be able to go and visit them. I wanted to make sure

I wouldn't have a problem finding the house, so I asked Peter.

Barry: "Can you help me find the house? I don't want to get lost."

Peter: "You won't get lost. All you have to do is go out the door, turn right and when you get to the corner, turn right again. You'll recognize the house."

I looked at John and asked if we were good.

John: "Oh yeah, we're great, but the next time I get a haircut, you'll have to answer one question for me. What's meatloaf?"

John and Peter walked out together. As they passed the window, they were talking and laughing. I have to admit it was nice to see John laughing but something outside caught my eye. As they crossed the street, I noticed it looked just like the cover of Abbey Road. Then it occurred to me that this was not the first time the view through my window had been different. When Gerty left, it looked like the Left Bank and Carlo seemed to depart into what appeared to be a small village in Italy. By this point, nothing in Heaven was a surprise anymore, and even though I wondered what was happening, at this point I was more interested in going to see my parents. I grabbed the broom and swept as fast as I could, looked in the mirror to make sure I looked presentable to Mom, and walked out the door (as giddy as a schoolboy) to face this new world for the first time.

When I got outside, I turned right, went to the corner, and turned right again, just like my dad and Peter said to do. When I came around the corner, there it was. The house I grew up in. Perfect in every way. I stopped for a moment to take a deep breath and walked up the walkway to the front door. It was the same doorbell I remembered. The door opened and there she was, so young and beautiful, like the pictures I used to look at on rainy days.

Mom: "Any trouble finding the house?"

Barry: "Really, Mom? How could I miss this house?"

Mom: "Oh good, come in. Dinner's almost ready."

Walking into my parent's house was like walking through a time portal. It not only looked exactly like I remembered it, but the smell of meatloaf also helped to make it more like home. I stood for a moment just looking at her and realized how much I had missed her. It was a no-brainer to go over to her and put my arms around her. I didn't want to let her go, but she broke the moment by saying she had better check the meatloaf. I laughed and followed her into the kitchen. I was back home.

Chapter IX

Hearing my mother's voice might be the greatest thrill I'd had since coming to Heaven. I didn't want to stop hearing it, so I told her about John Lennon and her meatloaf.

Barry: "Hey, Mom, I just cut John Lennon's hair and he asked me what meatloaf was. Can you imagine? I couldn't imagine going through life having never eaten your meatloaf."

She smiled and said, "That's very funny… Who's John Lennon?"

Barry: "Really, Mom? John Lennon? The Beatle."

Mom: "Oh yeah, we should save him some."

Barry: "I think he'd love that, but I don't know where he lives. Besides, what makes you think I'm gonna leave any? I'm starving! So, where's Dad?"

Mom: "He's in his workshop doing some final touchups on his new lampshade. I think you will be impressed. He's been working with Louis Tiffany on it. They've become good friends and Louis has taught him some tricks of the trade."

Barry: "So, how have you been, Mom?"

Mom: "Good, I guess, but I'm a little mad at God."

Barry: "You're mad at God? What did He do to make you mad?"

Mom: "He stole your dream. I remember how important it was to you. It was all you talked about. The least He could have done is wait a bit longer so you could enjoy it before He brought you here."

Barry: "Oh, don't be mad at Him for that. I think Dad was right. It was only a dream. Besides, I'm happy to be here in Heaven and especially with you and Dad."

Mom: "Well, I'm glad to hear that, and we're glad to see you too sweetheart."

Barry: "By the way mom, you look fantastic. I have to admit I was expecting you to be a lot older."

Mom: "That's one of my favorite things about living in Heaven. You get to pick how old you want to be. Some people like being really young and others like how they looked when they were older. It doesn't matter because no one feels the pain of aging and no matter how we look, we have the energy of a child."

Barry: "Well, you look great. Don't change a thing."

Just then, my father came in from his workshop, holding his new Tiffany lamp. It was long and rectangular with two lamps coming up from the base. The single stained-glass shade covered both lamps and was a series of red, white, and blue diagonal stripes – like a barber pole. Along one side was a smaller rectangular piece of soft white translucent glass with gold leaf letters that read "God's favorite barber."

Dad: "Here, son, this is for your shop."

Barry: "It's beautiful, Dad. I love it! I know exactly where to put it, and I will make sure everyone knows who made it."

Mom interrupted, as she did so often.

Mom: "Dinner won't be ready for a while. Why don't the two of you go sit in the living room and I will call you when it's ready. By the way, Barry, I invited someone to join us for dinner. I think you will be pleasantly surprised."

Barry: "Who?"

Mom: "Let's leave it as a surprise."

Mom loved teasing my curiosity, but I learned long ago, pursuing it would only be futile. Dad poured a couple glasses of wine and we went to the living room. We had just sat down when the doorbell rang.

Dad: "I'll get it, dear."

He went to the door and opened it. In walked the biggest surprise I could imagine.

Barry: "Ana?"

She was smiling and her smile served as a reminder of just how beautiful she was. We had met back in our early twenties, but it had been decades since I'd seen or spoken to her. She was the sister of my best friend's girlfriend, and when she was introduced to me, it was love at first sight. She quickly became my girlfriend. I remember thinking I had died and gone to Heaven. She was my Earth angel and now that she was here, she looked even more Heavenly.

There was one thing though. She was the first and only woman to break my heart. The pain was like nothing I had ever felt, and I decided to never feel that again. The fear of feeling that pain ever again was the reason I remained single for the rest of my life. But seeing her again, I found myself caught up in the same feelings I had back when I first met her. My fear of that pain seemed to blow away like dust in the wind. Just then, Mom came into the room.

Mom: "Dinner's ready. Hi, Ana, I'm so glad you could come over."

We all walked to the table and Mom sat her across from me so we could look at each other.

Ana: "How are you, Barry? I hope you don't mind me coming for dinner."

I was looking so deep into her beautiful brown eyes; I didn't even hear her question.

Mom, with a smile on her face, said, "Barry? Did you hear what Ana asked you?"

Barry: "I'm sorry, I was thinking how long it had been. What did you say?"

Ana giggled and blushed. "That's our Barry, always lost in his thoughts. I just asked how you were and if you minded me coming for dinner."

I grinned and said, "I'm doing great! And no, I couldn't be happier that you did."

The room went awkwardly quiet for a moment, so I jumped in.

Barry: "Have you been here in Heaven long?"

Ana: "Yeah, for a while now. I died in an auto accident in my early forties."

Finding myself without anything to say, I looked over to my mother just long enough to catch her looking down at her plate, smiling with a look of accomplishment. My mother loved Ana and was almost as heartbroken as I was when we broke up.

Barry: "That's funny, well, not funny, but ironic. I died in a car crash too. So, what do you do to keep yourself busy here?"

Ana: "I love to cook and I like to write. A perfect combination for a cookbook, but probably not a very good idea since no one eats in Heaven."

Barry: "But we're about to eat now."

Ana: "God understands how important sitting around the dinner table was to humans back on Earth and makes an exception occasionally up here, but we don't need food. In my case, because it's my passion, He allows me to cook for other people anytime I want. It beats spending the day lying around the house watching TV. Your mother told me that you became a barber. Is that what you do here in Heaven?

I didn't want to say I was a writer too because it would sound like I was competing and I wanted to show her my support for her book.

Barry: "Yeah, it is and I've had some very interesting clients since I got here. One of them is Gertrude Stein. Do you know who she is? She was the muse for some of the great writers of the early twentieth century. I could give her your book if you want some feedback on it."

Ana: "Oh yeah, I know who she is. Do you know her? Why am I not surprised? You always seemed to attract interesting people."

Barry: "Well, I don't really know her and not

sure I'd want to, but I would be happy to give her your book."

Dad: "Stein read something Barry wrote and said she saw talent."

Ana: "You write too? I would love to read it."

I shrugged and said, "It's a work in progress, but when I get somewhere with it, I'd love for you to read it too."

Mom: "By the way, Barry, Ana lives just across the street. Isn't that a coincidence?"

I remembered what my father told me at the shop. Everyone you love and loves you lives right around the corner. I thought to myself, Maybe it's not a coincidence, maybe it's a sign. But then, I could be wrong, so I just smiled with a mouthful of meatloaf and nodded in agreement.

I took another bite of the meatloaf and it was better than the first. It's been said that everyone thinks their mother makes the best meatloaf. Little did any of them know, my mother's was the best.

Barry: "Mom, the meatloaf is even more delicious than I remember."

I looked over at Ana.

Barry: "It may not be something fancy like saltimbocca, but I could eat this every day."

Ana: "It is delicious. It's the first time I've ever eaten meatloaf. My mom only cooked Argentinian food.

She glanced over at my mom.

Ana: "Maybe you could teach me to cook it and I could make it for Barry sometime."

That reminded me why she and I broke up. Her parents were from Argentina, and one day out of the blue, her father decided to move the rest of the family back there. After they were gone, she was always so sad and missed them terribly. I decided a perfect Christmas gift would be to give her a round-trip ticket to see them. I'll never forget I got big-time kudos for that gift and she flew off to Buenos Aires. The problem was, she never came back.

Mom: "If you think the meatloaf is good, wait until dessert. Ana made a tiramisu. I've never had tiramisu."

Barry: "That sounds great! Good tiramisu is very hard to make. You must be a very good chef."

Ana: "Not really, calling me a chef is a bit of a stretch. I did travel all over the world before I died and loved learning to cook from lots of the great chefs, but I think I would take your mom's meatloaf over any of their dishes. She has set a very high bar for me to reach."

While mom blushed, the rest of us shared a loving laugh. The whole time, I couldn't take my eyes off Ana. She was so beautiful and her smile lit up the room. I caught her sneaking a look at me a couple of times, but I acted like I didn't notice.

Barry: "Well, you are going to have to cook us something very exotic one day. Dad is a steak-and-potatoes man, but Mom and I will eat worms. I think it's time for dad to break out of his box a little, don't you think so, Mom?"

Ana: "I would love to, and I promise I won't make worms."

The room was full with laughter as Mom brought out the tiramisu and cut each of us a slice, but quickly turned quiet as we all ate. I was looking at Ana, Ana was looking at me, Mom was looking at the two of us and Dad looked down at his tiramisu.

Barry: "Oh no, Ana, you're wrong. You are a chef! This is Heavenly."

With their mouths full, Mom and Dad shook their heads in agreement.

Ana: "You are all so sweet. I'm glad you like it."

We finished it in a flash and moved to the living room. Dad pulled out his best cognac and poured each of us a glass. We must have sat and talked for hours. The whole time, it seemed she and I couldn't take our eyes off each other. I broke away just long enough to look over at my mother and she still had that smile of accomplishment on her face. Her smile brought me back to the moment, and I wondered how long I should stay there before I had to get back to the shop. I was thinking I better not push my first time out of the barbershop, when Ana said she should probably get going.

Barry: "I should too. I'll walk you home. It's on my way."

Ana: "I would love that."

Barry: "Mom, I can't tell you how great it is to see you again and you outdid yourself on the meatloaf. Grumpy, my lamp is fantastic, and I love it! I think you might have a future in it. Thank you so much."

Ana and I got up at the same time, and she followed me to the door. We both gave my Mom and Dad hugs, thanked them for dinner and she promised to have 'em over soon.

I grabbed the lamp, and the two of us walked out the door and down the walkway.

On the way over to my parent's house, I had been so excited to get there, I hadn't paid attention to my surroundings. Now walking beside Ana, my senses were acute, and I was seeing everything. The sky was as blue as I had ever seen and the temperature seemed perfect.

Barry: "What a gorgeous day."

Ana: "It's always like this here. I thought it would get boring after a while, but it never has. Blue skies and seventy degrees every day. I take a walk every afternoon for what seems like an hour and every time I go for a walk, the surroundings are different. It's crazy. One day I turn right at the corner and I'm in a beautiful park and the next day, the same walk is in a forest. If you like, we could go for a walk together one day soon."

Barry: "I would love that. We can turn right and let Heaven surprise us. By the way, you said you like to write. When the cookbook is done, do you have any other ideas for books?"

Ana: "I would love to write a romantic novel, but since there's no sex in Heaven, I'm not sure anyone would be interested in that either."

Barry: "Wait! There's no sex in Heaven?"

Ana: "No reason for it. There's no procreation, so no need for sex."

Barry, smiling: "Well, what fun is that?"

Ana: "It's actually fine. For some reason, people can feel the same pleasure from simply touching and kissing each other. At least, that's what I've been told. I haven't felt it yet. So far, there's been no one I wanted to share that with."

Barry: "Really? I would imagine there are a million men up here that would love to feel that with you."

Ana: "I guess I've just never met the right one."

Barry: "I guess when you think about it, no sex would keep things simpler. I was talking to John Lennon earlier and he'll be glad to hear that. He doesn't put much stock in sex."

Ana: "You spoke to John Lennon? How did that happen?

Barry: "He came in for a haircut. It was pretty amazing. I didn't know it was him at first. His hair and beard were so long, you couldn't see his face through it all. And, while I was cutting his hair, George Harrison popped in and they started singing together. Can you believe it? I got a private Beatles concert."

Ana: "That's amazing! What were they like?"

Barry: "Harrison was very laid back and cool. At first, John was kind of a recluse, but after George left, he opened up and we had a great conversation."

Ana: "Gertrude Stein, George Harrison, and John Lennon? Who else's hair have you cut?"

Barry: "Saint Peter, Lucifer, and oh yeah... Carlo Ponzi."

Ana: "Oh, I met Mr. Ponzi shortly after I got here. He helped me through a rough time, but, the rest... Exactly who are you, Barry Masters?"

I looked down, chuckled, and in a voice riddled with embarrassment, said, "I guess I'm God's favorite barber."

Ana smiled and said, "Well, you're my favorite barber too."

I don't know what got into me. I've always been

a shy man, but for some reason, I put the lamp under one arm and with my other hand, gently reached for hers. She wrapped her fingers around mine in approval. While we held hands, I remembered a movie where the main character said that when he took his wife's hand for the first time, he knew immediately that she was the one. That was how I was feeling. We didn't speak the rest of the way, but I noticed her looking at me out of the corner of my eye.

We walked up to her porch, stopped, and she turned in my direction, still holding my hand.

Ana: "Would it be all right if I stop by to see you at your shop?"

Barry: "Only if I can stop by and see you here."

Ana: "Anytime you'd like, please."

We looked into each other's eyes, and it felt like they had connected somewhere between us. Then, I did something so out of character. I put my hand on her cheek and leaned forward to kiss her, but I stopped halfway to see her reaction. She leaned forward too and with the softest lips I had ever felt, she kissed me. She placed her hand on my side and I could feel it trembling. I wanted to kiss her harder but thought this was perfect. Our lips separated and she smiled. In the history of smiles, this had to be the most perfect smile ever.

Then, for some reason, she looked over my

shoulder. I turned to see what she was looking at and there was Peter right behind me. With a tone of embarrassment for interrupting, he apologized and said someone was waiting for me in the shop. I took my hand away from her cheek, smiled, and quietly excused myself, telling her it wouldn't be long before I returned.

Peter and I crossed the street, heading back to the shop without speaking a word. Just before we turned the corner, he put his arm over my shoulder, looked back at Ana watching us walk away, smiled, and said, "Perfect."

I looked over my shoulder at her and replied, "Yeah."

Chapter X

As Peter and I turned the corner toward the shop, I noticed that now the street looked like Vienna in the 1920s. A very strange phenomenon that even my wildest imagination couldn't explain.

Barry: "Peter, I noticed that my shop's street keeps changing its appearance. It looked one way when Gerty was there and another when Carlo and John were getting their haircut. What's that about?"

Peter: "I hope you don't take this wrong, but even though you're God's favorite barber, He wants everyone to feel at home in Heaven. Your shop is on a public street and its appearance changes for whoever is there. But you're one of the lucky ones. You have your own special street just around the corner that never changes. Not many of us have that."

Since no one was on the street, I peeked through the shop window to see who was waiting with the hope that it might explain this metamorphose. Sitting in one of the mid-century chairs was a middle-aged man, medium height and lean, with a perfectly manicured beard. He had short brown hair with an ever-so-subtle combover. He didn't look like he needed either a haircut or a beard trim.

We entered the shop and Peter said, "Barry, this is Dr. Sigmund Freud. Sig, this is Barry."

Now it made sense. Freud stood up with purpose and shook my hand. His handshake was firm, but at the same time, therapeutic.

Barry: "It's a real honor to meet you, sir. How can I be of service to you?"

Peter: "Sig wants you to cut his hair like mine."

Barry: "Well, that won't be a problem."

Peter: "Great! Then I'll leave you to the business at hand."

I took the chair cloth and draped it around Freud and began combing through his hair to get a feel for it, but honestly, all I could think about was Ana. I couldn't get that kiss out of my mind and the way she held my hand. I also couldn't help but ask myself, was this what true love felt like? My consciousness was shocked back to reality by the thick Austrian accent of Freud's voice.

Sigmund: "Dear sir, did you hear what I asked?"

Barry: "I'm sorry, Dr. Freud, my mind was in another place. What did you ask?"

Sigmund: "I asked if you thought I would look good without a part."

Without a part was code for a combover. A feeble effort by many men who thought a handful of hairs combed across the top of their head would conceal their reality.

Barry: "Absolutely! It will look much better and won't take more than a few minutes."

Sigmund: "Well, I certainly hope you can keep your focus during that time. Are you all right?"

Barry: "Yes, sir! In fact, I'm more than all right. I just came from my parents and met, or should I say reunited with, a woman I haven't seen for decades. Now, I can't get her out of my mind."

Sigmund: "Well, when it comes to the mind, you couldn't have had a better client in your chair right now. What is this beautiful woman's name?"

Barry: "Ana, I mean Chana. Everyone calls her Ana."

Sigmund: "That's a beautiful name."

Barry: "She's a beautiful woman, but you know what, something is bothering me."

Sigmund: "Please, do tell me."

Barry: "We were talking as I walked her back home and she told me there's no sex in Heaven, and I can't wrap my head around that. Honestly, it's all I can think about."

Sigmund: "So, this is all about sex?"

Barry: "Not at all, but isn't the passion felt from making love a big part of a fulfilling relationship?"

Sigmund: "I believe that to be true, and it is as true here in Heaven as it was on Earth. The difference is, here in Heaven, sex isn't necessary to feel that passion. It can be experienced by a simple touch, a smile, or a kiss."

Barry: "Don't get me wrong, but as wonderful as it felt to hold her hand and kiss her, it didn't feel as good as I'm sure making love would."

Sigmund: "But it's still just sex. We're better off without it. Sex, with all its pleasure, is the most dangerous weapon in man's arsenal. Most people on Earth, as well as myself, believed sex was an expression of love, but in truth, it is used more as a weapon to deceive, control, and manipulate, rather than an expression of love."

Barry: "With all due respect to you sir, that's not a reason for throwing the baby out with the bathwater. I'm talking about making love, being connected to another person, physically, emotionally, and spiritually. To me, it's like tapping into higher consciousness. A Godlike consciousness and one would think that God would appreciate that, not get rid of it."

Sigmund: "Yes, I see your point, but remember, you can have sex without love and you can also have love without sex. The love of a parent or a child, or the love of your work, why not the love of another? And although I understand your reluctance to this thinking, in the end, we have to accept that here in Heaven, it is what God says it is."

I thought to myself, John Lennon would get along great with this guy. The two of them were cut from the same cloth. Both had such disdain for sex, but despite their credentials, I wasn't ready to give in to love without sex.

Barry: "I'm sorry, but I'm not willing to accept that. In the short time, I've been in Heaven, I've seen many flaws. I certainly don't have your expertise in the secrets of the heart and mind, but it seems to me that God may have dropped the ball on this one. To me, despite any logic, making love – sex – is not a weakness or a strength. It is an action that takes love to a higher place. It seems to me that getting rid of it makes as much sense as cutting off an arm to win a race."

Sigmund: "That's how I felt on Earth, but now that I'm here, things are different. I have always believed that the pleasure of love can only be achieved through an erotic connection of men's and women's genitalia, but what God did was take that sensation out of the equation. Let me ask you, at any point when you were with this special woman, did you ever feel anything in that region of your body?"

Barry: "Not really."

Sigmund: "Yet you appear to be very much in love with her."

I had to admit that he was right about that. On every first date I could remember, there was always a moment when I felt, at least, a bit of a sensation. Many times, I might have felt too much. But still, the question remained…why? Why did God take this intense joy we feel with another person away from us?

Barry: "Do you think, if man had obeyed the Bible regarding sex, God may have decided to keep it here in Heaven?

Sigmund: "The Bible? Haven't you learned anything since you got here? The Bible, and for the most part religion, is not God's work. They are man's feeble attempt at understanding Him. I admit it's very hard to make sense of the world without God, but it is very easy to imagine it without religion. Man doesn't need a whole Bible. God's message is one simple word… Love. Love Him and love thy fellow man. Regarding sex, I think God just looked at how man abused that precious gift he gave us and decided that the negatives outweighed the positives."

Since I found little I agreed with him on, I felt it best to concentrate on his hair. I had finished the top like he asked and decided I might as well freshen him up around the ears and neck. Besides, it would give him more time to continue this conversation to see if he could change my deeply entrenched mind. Then I thought there was nothing he could say that would do that, so I just changed the subject.

Barry: "You know, John Lennon of the Beatles was in here a little while ago. He and I had a very interesting conversation on this same subject. We decided that hate isn't the opposite of love, but rather fear is, and too many people on Earth are afraid of love or afraid to love and we wondered why God gave us fear. We talked about 'fearless' love and how great the world would be if we only had love void of fear. What do you think about that?"

Sigmund: "I'm not familiar with this gentleman, Mr. Lennon, but any love that man fears is not true love. I'll go a step further. God didn't create fear, man did. Fear is the accumulation of man's experiences, mistakes, and failures and it doesn't have to be his own. They can be those of someone close, like a parent, a sibling, or a good friend. And many times, this fear is tangible and it is set off by triggers that act as reminders of how things ended in the past. Obviously, no triggers were set off with this new lady of yours."

Barry: "Boy, are you right about that. When I would go on a first date, within fifteen minutes, triggers would start going off in my head. In the past, I would ignore them until I couldn't any longer. Sometimes that would happen after one or two dates. Other times it took me years to recognize them. But that's not the case with Ana. I didn't hear any triggers, just bells."

I had pretty much finished everything I could with the little hair he had. I always liked to cut hair with the customer's back to the mirror. I learned over the years that the process of watching me work in the mirror created too much angst. When I was done, I would turn them around. This time was no different. I brushed off Dr. Freud, turned him toward the mirror.

Barry: "So, what do you think?"

Sigmund: "Oh my, yes! It looks fantastic. My daughter will be so pleased. She is always on my case about my part.

I removed the chair cloth and he smiled even wider.

Sigmund: "I will have to thank Peter for suggesting I come here, and I want to thank you for a job very well done. I hope one day, I can meet this young woman of yours."

Just then there was a tap on the window and there, outside, was Ana. She motioned if it was okay for her to come in. I waved her in and then looked at Dr. Freud and said, "Stay right here, sir, and you will get to meet her. I would love for her to meet you too."

Ana came in and stopped for a moment, looking around in awe of the shop God had created for me.

Barry: "Ana, I'd like you to meet Dr. Sigmund Freud. Dr. Freud, this is Ana."

Ana: "It is such a privilege to meet you, Dr. Freud. You know I took a tour of your home in Austria a few years ago, and what a beautiful home it was."

Sigmund: "Why thank you, and might I say, you're as beautiful as I imagined, after speaking to this talented young man."

Ana blushed and said, "Dr. Freud, maybe you can answer this for me. What is it about Barry that invites so many famous and interesting people like yourself to come and sit in his barber chair?"

Sigmund: "I wondered that myself. He's a very smart young man, and I have enjoyed our conversation. Seems to me, he's much more than just a barber. It is obvious that he's a very special person, but you already knew that, didn't you?"

Ana: "Yes, I did."

Dr. Freud got up, turned toward Ana, smiled,

and slowly tipped forward in a proper gentleman's bow, then turned to me, thanked me for the haircut, and walked out the door.

Ana: "I may have to spend more time here in your shop. It must be so exciting to meet all these famous people. Do you ever wonder who will be next?"

Barry: "All the time, but I wonder sometimes if these people aren't all a part of some grand plan that God has put forth."

Ana: "If that were true and you could have anyone in history walk through your door next, who would it be?"

Barry: "Oh, that's easy. Mark Twain. Not only is he my favorite writer and his stories are way before their time, his wit and common sense are unmatched in the history of literature."

Ana: "I've only read Huckleberry Finn and Tom Sawyer, but I loved them and always thought I should read more of his work. What do you recommend?"

Barry: "It's so hard to choose, but one of my favorite books of his, is Pudd'nhead Wilson and a fun short story is Captain Stormfield's Visit to Heaven, but you can't go wrong with any of his works."

Ana took out a small notebook and wrote the names down and in her most innocent voice said, "I hope you don't mind that I came by. I was curious to see where you work. It's a beautiful shop."

Once again, I found myself mesmerized by her beauty. Her eyes were like fine Swiss chocolate. Her olive skin looked almost too soft to touch, and her smile. Oh, that smile. A smile that brought my world to a screeching halt. I snapped out of my deep thought just in time to respond to her.

Barry: "You are welcome anytime…all the time."

I smiled and Ana turned her head down to the left in embarrassment and blushed. That only validated my position that God had dropped the ball on sex. We sat on the two barber chairs talking and got lost in time. We laughed and talked about our lives, our loves, and our dreams. Throughout the conversation, she made me feel that everything I said was important and deserved her undivided attention. I was beginning to understand how my father felt about my mother. I was falling in love, but it was all moving so fast, maybe too fast? I worried I might scare her away, but she seemed so at ease, I quickly dismissed that thought.

I was about to ask her a question when the door flew open. There, with the light radiating from behind creating an almost angelic silhouette, was a man with thick, wavy white hair, a burly mustache that surrounded his mouth, and a three-piece suit that matched the color of his hair. There was no mistaking that face.

He stopped at the door and asked, "Was that Sigmund Freud I just saw leaving this establishment?" I answered yes and he said, "What a pompous quack! Anyway, I was told by Gertrude Stein I should come here if I wanted a good haircut. My name is –"

Before he could say his name, I interrupted, "I know who you are, Mr. Twain. I've seen hundreds of pictures of you."

Twain: "Good! Then you know how I like my hair cut." He looked over at Ana and said, "I'm sorry, am I interrupting?"

Ana looked at me in astonishment and looked back at Twain.

Ana: "Not at all, sir. We were just catching up."

We both got up, and I motioned him toward the chair. With one hand behind his back, he gracefully strolled over and sat down.

Ana: "I'd better go. I just remembered I have some very important reading to do."

She walked over to me, grabbed both my hands, and gave me a kiss on the cheek. I have to admit, there was a sensation I had never felt before from a kiss.

Ana: "I hope you will stop by soon, Barry. I'll make you dinner and we can continue catching up.

Barry: "Very soon, I promise."

While still holding my hands, she looked over her shoulder at Twain.

Ana: "It's a rare privilege to make your acquaintance, Mr. Twain."

Twain: "Trust me, the privilege of meeting such a beautiful woman trumps all others."

She leaned forward to my ear and whispered, "This is too strange. I want to hear all about it later." She let go of my hands, turned, and walked out. But as she passed the window, she tapped on it again and threw me one last kiss.

Twain: "It appears to me that you are one very lucky man."

Barry: "I'm beginning to think luck has nothing to do with it."

Chapter XI

Twain sat back looking very stoic with his head and back in straight alignment, holding an unlit cigar and seemingly in deep thought. I draped the cloth over him thinking this could be the most disappointing moment since coming to Heaven. I had spent most of my adult life wondering what it would be like to meet him, and now that I had him sitting right in front of me, I felt resigned to the fact that I might never learn anything more than I already knew.

Just then, out of the blue, he spoke with a tone of disdain, "Where did you get that idea about luck? From that poor excuse for a headpeeper, Freud?"

Barry: "No, not at all. I've been thinking that for

a while. Can I ask, why do you dislike him so much?"

Twain: "His hypotheses are rubbish, he's pompous and an opportunist. If he were alive on Earth today, I think the term they would use is shock jock."

Barry: "I have to admit, I disagreed with most everything he said, but I found myself in awe of him."

Twain: "Of course you did. That's his strength. He uses five-dollar words where dime store words are sufficient. The id and the superego, what bric-a-brac. The Chinese knew that at least five hundred years before him. They called them the Yin and Yang. Even Sir Isaac Newton understood it two hundred years ago and called it his third law. Trust me, it's not hard to make the case that Freud is nothing more than a fraud."

Barry: "That's pretty harsh, Mr. Twain. I understand what you're saying, but he is a famous doctor of the mind."

Twain: "You mean infamous. He's no better than a traveling tent preacher except he takes your money with promises that he has the power to heal your mind. So, what did you talk about?"

Barry: "Sex, or the lack thereof here in Heaven. He tried to give me some cock and bull that it has been replaced by a smile, a touch, and a kiss. I'm not buying it."

Twain: "Nor should you. There is nothing, I'm

aware of, that could ever replace the feeling one gets from the act of lovemaking. Of course, in the grand ol' business of horse-trading, I have never been one to examine the mouth of a gifted horse, so I feel compelled to take the side of God's celestial decree in order to remain in His good graces. I'm sure He has His reasons and besides, at my advanced age, it makes little difference to me. You, on the other hand, and especially after seeing your lovely lady, have much more reason to question His decision. Have you asked God about this troubling dilemma?"

Barry: "No, I haven't met Him yet, and I don't understand that either. He supposedly brought me to Heaven to cut His hair, and it seems like I'm cutting every famous person's hair but His. And things are very suspicious. Nothing seems random. Take you, for instance. Ana, that lovely lady, asked me whom I would most like to sit in my chair and I said you. Just a minute later, you appeared at the door. Does that sound like a coincidence?"

Twain: "I'm very flattered you said me, but let us hope it is a coincidence. Things are so much more interesting that way. But I can't say with any sense of certainty, whether it was coincidence or some sort of a devious plot. I was sent by my dear friend, Gertrude Stein. I doubt she carries any deceitful intentions toward you. She seems to like you and even praised you as a writer. By the way, I'll apologize now for not asking if I can read your writing, but I learned a long time ago not to read another author's work. At worst, I would be envious and at best, I would regret having to tell you to remain in this barbarous profession."

Barry: "You don't like barbers?"

Twain: "As I wrote in an essay once, barbers are an unholy invention of Satan, and all their instincts are cruel and revolting." He paused and with what I would suspect to be a rare smile, finished by saying, "Now, get to the job at hand and prove me wrong,"

I started to look at the geometrics of his haircut so I could do the same thing, but shorter. I planned to only cut a short amount of hair off, with the understanding that if he wanted more cut, I would be able to oblige. As I had said over the years, it's easy to cut more off, but I haven't yet mastered the art of making it longer. Besides, having to cut more off would only allow me more time to talk with him. The room went quiet again as he returned to his picturesque pose. Not being someone who enjoys the sound of silence, I struck up the conversation again.

Barry: "I think it's safe to say, you have a very grim opinion of man's impression of God and Heaven."

Twain: "And for good reason. It lacks any common sense. In fact, God once told me that my Letters from the Earth was on point. He told me that He has little or no interest in most of what man thinks He is, or what they think He's responsible for."

Barry: "I admit, Letters is one of my favorites, although I must admit, under the current circumstances, I have some trepidation saying that about a story that has such a negative view of God."

Twain: "It's not about God; it's about religion, and I know He believes that to be true based on the simple fact that I wouldn't be here if He thought otherwise. He asked me once why I thought humans were so devoted to their Bible."

Barry: "What did you tell Him?"

Twain: "I told Him it didn't matter. As long as He didn't offer his own manifesto, man would reach for whatever was on the shelf, be it right or wrong. The Bible was written by man, for man. Its purpose is to legitimize his fears and justify his desires. Especially to the mass who lacks the interest or ability to critically think and prefer to be handed something rather than make even the slightest effort to discover it for themselves. Throughout my travels around the world, that has never been clearer than in America. It is common practice for Americans to express their unwavering love for liberty, but most have willingly made the sacrifice of that liberty to be told what to do by what they think is the Word of the Almighty."

Barry: "What did He say to that?"

Twain: "He agreed with me, but His reluctance was due to His commitment, or maybe I should say, His compulsion that we all have free will."

Barry: "Well, I'm just a simple barbarian, but it would seem to me that leaving the Bible as is would only negate man's free will. I mean, fewer rules would have to be better than what it is now. Don't you think?

Twain: "That's exactly what I told Him. The Bible, as it is written, is vague and at the mercy of charlatan interpretations for personal gains, whether that be power or riches."

Barry: "What did He say to that?"

Twain: "He agreed and asked me if I would be interested in writing a new one. He thought bringing some common sense to the fold might be exactly what was needed, but I declined."

Barry: "Why? It seems to me that would be the culmination of an already iconic career. You could call it, The New Bible According to Twain (Edited by God)."

For the first time since he sat down, he laughed out loud.

Twain: "Good title, but I have no interest in dealing with such responsibility. I'm a simple humorist and my stories are written with the understanding that I dimly suspect there is nothing funny about them. But then, man's sense of humor is as flawed as his beliefs. It is based on the pain of others. He laughs only when he feels superior to the target of his laughter, but he finds nothing funny when he becomes the subject of that quip. It is not hard to defend the argument that the humorist is the loneliest person on the Earth. I know it to be true, firsthand. Far before Haley's comet returned for me and delivered me here, I had worn out my welcome on Earth."

Barry: "The last thing Gertrude Stein told me was that my writing should be honest, but you paint a rather ugly portrait of the honest writer."

Twain: "And for good reason. Man, as much as he claims to be, has never truly appreciated honesty. He believes, in his heart, that honesty is the best policy, but he spends his entire life living beyond arm's reach of it. I'm a sardonic writer. My friends, although loyal, have always kept a safe distance from me out of fear that they may become the next victim of my cynicism. A cruel and unjust reward for those who write with a razor-thin pen, but I learned to accept my punishment because of my inability to be anything else.

Barry: "But it seems anything less than that honesty wouldn't work for God's purpose."

Twain: "Quite right young man, but my temptation for mockery would not serve His needs. And quite frankly, age has dulled my pen, much like the scissors of an old barbarian."

He smiled as he went back to his statuesque pose, but his eyes gave away his deep thought. I was moving along on his haircut when he motioned for me to stop.

Twain: "I was thinking. Gertrude seems to think you have some real talent as a writer and after talking to you, I can see why. You have the thirst."

Barry: "What thirst is that?"

Twain: "That rare thirst for the question, rather than the answer. Probably a result of being a barber, but it is also the most important quality of a good writer. Most writers tell their readers what to think, but great writers ask them to think. They don't just feed the reader; they provide a hunger. Although I've never read a word you've written, talking to you makes me think you are, or at least could be, one of those writers. Maybe you are the one to write God's manifesto, but I will defer that to my dear friend Gertrude and the Almighty."

All I could do was laugh out loud. Now, in my line of work, one found out quickly just how contagious laughter was, so when I broke out laughing at what he said, it was only a matter of time before Twain started laughing. His laughter made me laugh more, and it became a snowball rolling down a hill.

It felt so good to laugh, I could barely bring myself to stop. Between the wonderment and my curiosity of this new world I had found myself in, I had little time to enjoy the simple pleasure of a good laugh and it was an even further thing from my mind to think I would ever be here laughing with my idol... but here I was. And what made it even funnier was the fact that I suspected Mr. Twain had no idea what we were laughing at.

Twain: "What are we laughing at?"

Barry: "I don't know what you're laughing at, but I'm laughing at your suggestion that I write God's manifesto."

Twain: "I'm glad it brought you such joy, but I was serious. Like me, I see a common-sense approach to your thinking, but minus the sarcasm."

Barry; "Thank you for such high praise, but I'm barely able to spell sarcasm. Anyway, we drifted from the topic at hand. Sex in Heaven!"

Twain: "Ah yes, sex in Heaven. Since you claim to be a fan of Letters, I'm sure you remember I had a lot to say about sex in that. But my opinion and experience with it here...now, in Heaven, can best be described to be only as theoretical as my good friend Nicola Tesla's explanation of wireless electricity. Having said that, if sex was intended to be an expression of love between a man and a woman, then why did God limit most men's biological clock to only a handful of years, while giving women a timeless ability? Under those conditions, one could argue that promiscuity would be the only expected result. Men seek it out so they can experience its pleasure as often as possible in their briefly competent time while women reach out to younger partners to enjoy it far beyond the ability of their significant other to perform to their satisfaction."

He stopped for a moment to gather his thoughts and take a breath.

Twain: "Also, it seems to me that God would have to be ignorant to the pleasures men and women get from different acts of sex since He has never experienced it Himself and He may not understand that His rules are nothing more than a ball and chain around their necks. Humans can do this, as long as they don't do that, leaving them in a precarious position of deciding between passion and virtue. Nevertheless, it is acutely apparent that the reason for His suspension of sex, be it cruel or loving, can only be answered by Him. I can only hope, especially for you in your current circumstances, that He has plugged this hole with something of equal value."

Barry: "I certainly hope so too. I never truly got to feel that true passion when I was on Earth. Now that I might be in that position, it appears to have been snatched from my grip. Can I ask you another question, Mr. Twain?

Twain: "Please, call me Sam. Of course, what is it?

Barry: "What would be the one question you would like to ask God if you could ask Him anything? I think it's obvious what I would ask, but what intrigues you about this grand experiment?"

Twain: "God relishes questions from His children, but when the purposed question is to criticize, His patience is as thin as a sail made of tissue paper in a squall. It has been said that man was created in God's image, and man's pride is the most fragile of all his emotions, so one can only suspect the same is true for God. Having said that, I think I would ask Him why free will is so important to him. On the rare occasion when a man is positioned to use his free will, he seems to always choose the perceived path of the greatest pleasure over the path of compassion. In truth, a wise man is suspicious of free will and he isn't the only one. Look at the angels. Lucifer used his free will, tells a joke, and God throws him out of Heaven. It didn't take long for the rest of the angels to fear, instead of relish their free will. I'm just a simple man, but I don't believe that you can offer man free will, without some guidelines. Especially if you punish him for using it. It can't work that way. All that happens is no one will use it."

Barry: "You just said that God doesn't like criticism, yet here you are saying His plan is flawed. Don't you worry about His reaction?"

Twain: "I didn't say it's flawed. I'm saying it's incomplete. You can't appreciate or play the game of baseball without any rules, but if the rules are created by the players, they will never hold themselves accountable. All the more reason for a true divine manifesto.

As far as risking my existence, I have spoken these words to Him and His reaction was to listen with eyes wide open. I think He knew this well before I spoke of it and is not averse to my exhortation. It is my opinion that He is most likely working on it as we speak.

Barry: "That would make sense. After all, He asked you to write His manifesto and John Lennon told me that he had been approached to be His prophet. It would appear He is aware of these problems and is searching for solutions to them."

Twain: "To find the right person for such duties, I'm sure, requires a tremendous amount of vetting. And if He is successful in finding someone, He must then convince that person to take on what could only be called a suicide mission. At best, it would be of great sacrifice to that person. Let us not forget what Jesus went through. Anyone less than The Son of

God would experience man's greatest scorn."

Barry: "So, why not use Jesus again? After all, the Bible speaks of His return."

Twain: "Jesus is an innocent. He could bring the message, live by it, but history shows us His inability to close the deal. God's message was simple. Love Him and love your neighbor. A nuance lost on mankind. Man can't accept something so simple. Besides, I'm sure his confidence was quite shaken after his last visit to Earth. No, Jesus isn't a candidate to be the messenger. It has to be someone stronger. Most of all, it must be someone with very thick skin. That alone would leave him off the list."

By this time, I had pretty much lost my focus regarding his haircut, but years of experience had taught me I could do it in my sleep. So, I finished the first draft of his haircut, took a final look at it, and turned him around toward the mirror for his opinion of my work. As much as it was important to me that he'd be pleased, there was a part of me that hoped I had done something wrong. I anxiously wanted more time to talk with him, but sadly, when he looked into the mirror, the expression on his face told me he was pleased.

Twain: "Since I have held nothing but disdain for all of my previous barbers, I am embarrassed to admit that you have set aside my lifelong adage. Kudos to our Lord for picking you to be His favorite barber."

Now, if someone had told me that I had just won a million dollars, I'm sure, my reaction would not have been any more enthusiastic than it was at that moment. I removed the cloth and he rose from the chair, but this time with a smile on his face.

Twain: "My friend Nicola will be so pleased to know I have found someone whose talents are equal to our own. You are not only the finest of all in your profession, but you have a great talent for bringing people out from themselves. In your own quiet way, you motivate and stimulate. It's been a pleasure spending this time with you and I look forward to our next sojourn."

Barry: "This has not only been the highlight of my time here, it has been the highlight of my life. Thank you for your kind words and I, too, will be here anxiously waiting for our next meeting."

With that, he left with that one arm neatly tucked behind his back just like when he entered. The moment he left, I grabbed my notebook and began to write. I didn't know if I could remember all we spoke about, but as I began to write, it all seemed to come back. After I finished writing, all I could think about was how much I was looking forward to Ana reading it. Despite the mentors and muses, I had the privilege to meet here so far, her opinion was the most important to me.

Since no one had told me when to work, I figured I would take a break from cutting hair and visit her. I hoped she would be as excited to see me as I would be to see her. I cleaned up the shop and myself, grabbed my notebook, put a sign on the door that read "Back in a few," and headed for around the corner.

Chapter XII

Just as I shut the door behind me, a boyish-looking man with overgrown shaggy hair walked up and asked me if I could cut his hair. Although my desire to see Ana made me hesitate for a moment, I realized I might miss a great opportunity for my writing if I said no, and I didn't think she would mind waiting a bit longer. So, I opened the door and invited him in.

As I walked back through the door, I couldn't help but think, Wouldn't it be a hoot if this was God? His appearance was not what I would expect God to look like, but little of what had happened since I got here had met my expectations. He wasn't tall, a bit frail, with a baby face that only a mother could love.

His horn-rimmed glasses only added to his aura of a diffident youth as he sat in the chair most uncomfortably, leaning on one arm. I felt a bit nervous at the fact that at some point, I might have to ask him to sit up straight so I could cut his hair right, but for the moment, I simply put the chair cloth over him and began to comb through his hair.

I introduce myself and he replied that he had already deduced that from the sign in the window. I asked him his name and he said, "Stephen."

Barry: "So Stephen, what do you do here in Heaven?"

Stephen: "I'm a confrontationist. I question things."

Barry: "So, who do you confront?"

Stephen: "Whoever needs correction."

Barry: "And how do you do that?"

Stephen: "I see the problem and try to ask the right question. My good friend Albert Einstein once said, 'Question everything,' and he's right, but too many ask the wrong question, and that only leads to the wrong answer. I take great pride in the fact that I ask the right question."

Barry: "So, all your questions are right? That's impressive."

Stephen: "Well, not all of them, but most. When I was on Earth, I questioned the existence of a God and after spending a great deal of my life searching through the evidence, I finally concluded there wasn't enough to determine the existence of a deity. Judging by our current circumstance, I think it's safe to say that was an example of bad questions."

Barry: "And that didn't upset God? I mean, I understand questioning religion, but God Himself?"

Stephen: "Well, I'm still here. As a Shia Imam once said, when proven wrong, the wise man will correct himself and the ignorant will keep arguing. I was wrong, but my intent was not to doubt but to conclude. He loves His creation to question when the intent is to understand. One of the most important things God gave to man was that ability to question. When I was a scientist on Earth, I devoted my life to the question. Why, where, what, when, and most importantly, how."

Barry: "What kind of scientist were you?"

Stephen: "I was a theoretical physicist and cosmologist. I studied the stars."

Barry: "I'm just a barber, but I have always had a place in my heart for the stars. I even read Hawking's A Brief History of Time."

Stephen: "What did you think of it?"

Barry: "I'm not really sure if I understood it. Science at that level requires a mind with great imagination. A person that can recognize a single tree amidst a forest. Did you read it?"

Stephen: "Yes, a few times."

Barry: "Did you understand it?"

With a calm voice of affirmation, he said, "I think so."

Barry: "Well, since you wrote it, Mr. Hawking, I would hope you understood it."

He laughed as if he had been caught with his hand in the cookie jar and said, "So, you know who I am."

Barry: "I didn't at first, but it didn't take long. I just wanted to see where our conversation would lead. I do have to say that I'm glad you no longer have to suffer from your disability."

Stephen: "There's no doubt that there were times when my physical limitations were an obstacle, but most of the time, I felt a great appreciation that despite them, I was able to imagine, question, and formulate ideas. Knowing my condition, I think you can understand why I questioned God's existence, but obviously, that question has been answered."

Barry: "I would imagine that most of your questions have been answered now."

Stephen: "I can see why you would think that, but to be honest, I have more questions now than I ever did on Earth. Science is like a snowball rolling down the hill. The more you know, the more questions there are."

Barry: "Did you answer the question of why

you're here in Heaven?"

Stephen: "At first, no, but soon after, it all made sense. It was my reward for being loyal to science despite all the obstacles God put in front of me and being loyal to science is being loyal to God. One could say with assurance that I was a modern-day scientific Job. No gift to man is more precious to God than science. It relieves Him from the burdens man places on Him and provides mankind with the tools to make their own lives better."

Barry: "My curiosity is overflowing. Why would you have more questions now than on Earth? I mean, can't you just ask God?"

Stephen: "What makes you think God has all the answers? This is all new to Him too. He created our universe and the Heavens, but He is very aware that they are far from perfect. He's changing it all the time. Science calls it evolution, and He expects us to study it and suggest to Him how it can be made better."

Barry: "Well, if there's a suggestion box, I have one."

Stephen: "What would that be?"

Barry: "Why did He take sex away from man here in Heaven? I understand the negatives, but couldn't you as a scientist suggest to Him a better solution than abolishing it altogether?"

Stephen: "But has He abolished it altogether? I mean what if the factors that bring us to that point are simply different than they were on Earth? On Earth, most of us could be aroused by something as simple as a photograph or a thought. What if here, in Heaven, the conditions are more specific? You know, despite my condition, sex wasn't above my pay scale. After all, I did have three children and I don't remember them coming from divine intervention. But when I ask myself why God would do this, I can't seem to come up with a good answer. My friend Albert says God doesn't play dice with His universe, but I disagree with him. I believe that He does, but sometimes He throws the dice where they can't be seen."

Barry: "I hope you're right. I have never felt like this about another person and it would seem like a Shakespearean tragedy if she and I couldn't fully express our feelings. Of course, I'm taking for granted that she feels the same way, but I'm pretty sure she does."

Stephen: "As I said, all I can tell you is what my good friend Albert said: 'Question everything.' Questions are the path to understanding and understanding to knowledge, but if you can't find the answers to your questions and still want to know, then you should ask God."

Barry: "I would, but I haven't met Him yet."

Stephen: "Yet you're His favorite barber? How can that be?"

Barry: "That, Mr. Hawking, is the question of questions. I don't understand what is going on here. The people who have come into the shop are so interesting and have opened my eyes to a whole new world of thinking, but the most important patron seems to be missing in action."

Stephen: "Maybe He's just not ready to talk to you, or you aren't ready to talk to Him."

Barry: "You seem to have a close relationship with God. What's He like?"

Stephen: "He's a curious being. He loves who He is, but man's impression of who He is can bewilder, humor, and sometimes anger Him. Of course, some of that is of His own doing. The thing that angers God most, is man's reluctance to use the gift of questions He has so generously given him. No other creature on Earth has been given this precious gift, yet most humans seem to have no interest in asking any questions, let alone the right ones."

Barry: "What do you mean by the right questions?"

Stephen: "Most humans tend to ask questions that serve to only validate what they already believe to be true and have no interest in crossing that line. God is dumbfounded at mankind's obsession to cling on for dear life to what is presented to them and fears going beyond that. Take, for instance, one of God's strangest creatures, the kangaroo. When Noah's ark finally rested atop Mount Ararat, this strange creature began a seven-thousand-mile pilgrimage across deserts, through jungles, and overseas, to its homeland, yet in over thirty-five hundred years since that migration, not one piece of evidence has ever been found to prove this trek. The right question would be how did they get back, but man doesn't concern himself with that question. He is willing to blindly follow his faith that the Bible is the Word of God, but if one is willing to accept the story of Noah and the flood as nothing more than an allegory, then the right question should be, how much of the rest of the Bible is factual?

Questions are the foundation of science, and where would mankind be today if not for science? If we were incapable of asking questions, nothing would be discovered, yet many think questions are the devil's work. And even those who believe questions are a gift from God, can get it wrong. It's been said that there is no such thing as a bad question. That's nothing more than poppycock. Most questions are bad questions."

Barry: "So give me an example of a bad question."

Stephen: "A bad question? Okay, what if we were invaded by soldiers from the future? A bad question is why are they here? They're soldiers; we know why they're here. You don't use soldiers for diplomatic missions. That's what I refer to as a rear-view mirror question. It only answers what we already know. The right question to ask is how can we prevent more soldiers from coming and defeat those that are here?"

Barry: "Is that why you're here? To ask God good questions?"

Stephen: "I'm not here to just ask Him questions, I exist to ask all questions that need to be asked. I'm a scientist and we are the most prized possession in God's grand plan. We create the tools needed to expand mankind's free will. We created the wheel, we found electricity, and we constantly created technology to make man's life better and longer. Science is responsible for all those things. Not God, science, and that's the way He wants it!

"Regarding your question about sex? It's not a very good question. The right question is why did He tether procreation to this expression of love called sex? If He wanted man to feel such great pleasure, why not do it in a standalone way? I once asked Him why He created sex in the first place. I suggested that sex should be either an act of pleasure or an act of procreation, but not both. Putting them together only confused man."

Barry: "What did He say? "

Stephen: "He thought about it for a moment and

simply replied, 'Good question.'"

Barry: "So, He admitted He might have been wrong?"

Stephen: "That, in itself, is not a surprise. Science shows us that perfection doesn't exist. The world is in constant motion, and it's a never-ending process of small changes. What makes sense today may not be right tomorrow. Of course, many answers are beyond human understanding. For example, the universe we can see is expanding, but the universe, as a whole, is shrinking. In five billion years, the Sun will run out of hydrogen and at that point will expand and vaporize the Earth. These kinds of theories are beyond man's imagination and quite frankly his interest. The concept of infinity, or eternity, is also well beyond the scope of the average man. Only a few humans can truly fathom endlessness, whether it be in the form of energy, gravity, time, or the existence of an eternal Heaven (if indeed Heaven is eternal)."

Hawking smiled with a compassionate smile and asked me if I was overwhelmed yet.

Barry: "I think I understand your point, even if I don't understand everything you said. Man is confined within a gated environment that only extends as far as his eyes can see. Beyond the gate lies many of the answers we are looking for. That may not be your point, but at least, that's how I feel. I am the first to admit that my imagination cannot go very far beyond my existence."

Stephen: "That makes you human, but don't feel bad about that. The only difference between you and me is our imaginations. Not that mine is better than yours; it's just different. I can't think beyond my existence any further than you. The difference is I am a man of science and you are a man of letters. Your questions relate to the why, while mine relates to the how."

I had to say, this wasn't the conversation I was expecting. Of course, none of my conversations here in Heaven had been. As I started the final touches of his haircut, I found myself pondering one last question.

Barry: "So are there any questions you are afraid to ask God?"

Stephen: "There are thousands, but there is a good reason why. If we are to believe that man was made in His image, we must take into account that His patience is like our own, a tightly taut twine. One never knows exactly when it will break. I don't want to risk being responsible for His loss of confidence in free will over something that may very well be within my comprehension, but I haven't yet seen for myself."

Barry: "Well, if you could ask Him one question

without that risk, what would it be?"

Stephen: "Oh, that's easy. If God created us, who created God? Even though I'm nothing more than a precocious inquisitor, my steadfast belief in infinity tells me that all doesn't stop at His feet. To be more precise, it doesn't stop."

Barry: "So, you're saying that God has a God?"

Stephen: "And that God has a God, but keep in mind that this is nothing more than a hypothesis. A product of my limited imagination. As I said, most people's imagination only goes as far as they can see, and they are unwilling to visualize beyond that out of the fear of being wrong. That fear limits their scope and best explains why man is satisfied to be told what to think and do. What they don't understand is that science is predicated on failure. What is thought to be today's laws of nature, will be tomorrow's folly. The Sun revolving around the Earth, the Earth being flat, or it is the only inhabited planet in the universe are all examples of the limitations of man's imagination. But man can't be blamed for being so narrow-minded. As you said, he lives in a world of walls. He is born and he dies, but if a man is lucky enough, like you and I, to wind up here in eternity, his scope broadens. But despite living in this eternal world, man still fears stepping out beyond the limits of his perception. Only men of science and letters are willing to boldly leap over that wall without fear of what might be on the other side."

Barry: "So then why are you afraid to ask Him this question?"

Stephen: "I'm not really afraid. I just haven't gone far enough in my own studies to ask Him. Keep in mind, more important than the answer to a question, are the questions created from that answer. At some point, science no longer has the information or vision to answer the questions. At that point, I will ask Him."

Barry: "Well, if it means anything, I think your hypothesis has merit, and I've enjoyed listening to you. I wish I could understand more of what you're saying."

Stephen: "Don't underestimate yourself. I can see in your eyes that you understand more than you give yourself credit for. You are truly a man of letters, and I'm sure that's why God picked you to be his barber."

I thanked him for the kind words, removed the cloth, and asked him if he liked the haircut. He said he was very happy with it but enjoyed our conversation even more. I laughed and told him I considered him to be my favorite haircut so far and that I wish I could have taken one of his classes on Earth. I saw his boyish face blush, as he said, "Remember, science tells us how the universe can exist, but it's men of letters, like yourself, that tell us why the universe goes to all the bother of existing."

He walked out the door, but as he walked past the window, he turned and gave me a short two-finger salute. As he went out of sight, I saw Peter walking by. I rushed over to the window and tapped on it and motioned for him to come in.

Barry: "Peter, I don't understand my hours here. Do I get breaks and when?"

Peter: "You can take a break anytime you want. I suspect that you want to go visit that lovely lady."

Barry: "I sure do. I was about to earlier and Stephen Hawking came in for a haircut."

Peter: "Great! He is one of God's favorite children. Did you enjoy your time with him?"

Barry: "Immensely, but I do want to visit Ana. How do I know when I should return?"

Peter: "Return when you want. Your barbering is not a job. It's a gift from God, but I know she is very important to you too. Take all the time you want with her. After all, this is Heaven. Everything here is a gift from God and since it's eternal, haircuts can always wait."

I thanked him and he left with that familiar smile of accomplishment. I picked up my notebook to write down my time with Stephen. I worried that

I would not be able to transcribe our conversation with accuracy, so I put a disclaimer at the beginning saying that everything I write is from memory and shouldn't be taken as literal. I swept up the shop and rushed out, hoping my plan to visit Ana wouldn't be interrupted by anyone else.

Chapter XIII

I think it's safe to say, my overall appearance had never been, or at least seldom been, unappealing to the eyes of most women. Although I would never claim to belong on the cover of some fashion magazine, I never had a problem finding very attractive women willing to submit to the limited charms I had been blessed with. Looking back, I have to say, with some shame, that most of my relationships were nothing more than two ships passing in the night, and in almost every relationship, I kept my heart safely tucked away. All, except with Ana.

Ana wasn't my first girlfriend but the first and only woman that stole and broke my heart. We were young and very much in love. In Ana's case, maybe too young. When her parents moved back to Argentina, she was so afraid of being far from her family and alone that she was forced to choose between me or them and I lost.

As I approached her home, I couldn't help but remember what my father had said. Everyone you love and who loves you is right around the corner. And there was her home, right there, around the corner. I walked up the front stairs to her door and rang the bell. The door opened and there she was smiling with a look of anticipation.

Ana: "I'm so glad you're here. I haven't stopped thinking about what happened and I've been dying to hear all about it. That was the strangest thing I've experienced since coming to Heaven."

Barry: "It was strange, wasn't it? I brought it up to Twain and he couldn't explain it. He told me that Gertrude Stein had sent him over, but I'm beginning to think everything that has happened to me here is part of some divine plan."

Ana: "Well, come in and I'll make you something to eat and you can tell me all about it."

She took my hand and walked me into the kitchen. She motioned for me to have a seat at the table, opened a bottle of wine, and poured two glasses. She handed me one and started preparing dinner.

Barry: "So, what are you making?"

Ana: "Well, since your father isn't here, I thought I would cook some worms."

She laughed at the look of uncertainty on my face.

Ana: "Don't worry, I didn't have time to go out in the garden and dig any up. So, you're getting my favorite Argentinian dish. It's called locro. It's like a South American gumbo with squash, beans, corn, papa chola, and meat that's seasoned in my own special way."

Barry: "I'm impressed. When did you get interested in cooking? I recall you couldn't boil water back when I knew you."

Ana: "I guess it started when I was living in Argentina. It started as a way to pass time, but after a while, it became a passion of mine and I traveled the world to learn all sorts of cuisines, but that's not important now. I want to hear all about Mr. Twain."

Barry: "I don't know where to start. After you left, he got very quiet, and I thought I may never get to ask him anything, but all of a sudden, he opened up."

She threw all the ingredients into a pot, seasoned, stirred, put the lid on, and joined me at the table.

Ana: "It won't take long, nothing up here ever does. So, go on, what did you talk about?"

Barry: "There's so much and I don't want to forget any of it. Wait! I know what I'll do. I'll be right back."

With that, I jumped up, ran out the door and

back to the shop, and grabbed my notebook. When I got back to her house, I turned to the Twain chapter. Out of breath, I handed it to her and said, "It's all there!"

Ana took it and began to read.

Ana: "Did you write this?"

Barry: "Yeah, does it make any sense?"

Ana: "Absolutely! Can I read some more?"

Barry: "Read all you want."

She turned to the next page.

Ana: "You mean you cut Stephen Hawking's hair after Twain's? Who are you, Barry Masters?"

Barry: "I guess I'm God's favorite barber, who likes to write."

Ana: "No... You're a writer that just happens to be God's favorite barber. Reading this makes me feel like I was standing right next to you."

I smiled and took a sip of wine to clear the frog in my throat. I was sure now that something was going on between us. Her eyes followed everything I did, like everything I did was special. No woman had ever done that before. I took another sip of wine.

Barry: "Don't let your locro burn."

Ana: "No reason to worry about that. Nothing up here burns, but that's probably because no one I know up here cooks...except me (and your mom). Cooking is my only personal evil pleasure and thanks to Mr. Ponzi, God has been generous enough to allow those close to me to enjoy my cooking. I hope you'll enjoy it."

With that, she grabbed two placemats and silverware and put them on the table across from each other. She lit a candle and centered it strategically on the table where it would not be between us. She went back to the stove, stirred it one last time, and filled two bowls. It smelled incredible. She placed one of the bowls in front of me.

Ana: "Dinner is served. Bon appétit."

I picked up the spoon and modestly filled it with the locro and sipped without a sound. The flavor was as rare a treat as Ana herself. The flavor of my second sip might have been even better. A multitude of flavors unfolded in my mouth as I savored each spoonful.

Barry: "This is unbelievable! What motivated you to become a chef?"

Ana: "Oh, I'm no chef. I just like to cook."

Barry: "You're more than a cook. I've never tasted anything this good."

Ana: "My mother always said, if you're going to do something, do it right."

Barry: "Then, your mother should be very proud of you."

Ana: "Would you like some more, some dessert,

or both? You can't get fat in Heaven."

Barry: "I don't know how much more I could eat. I'll try some dessert. After this locro, I would eat a mud pie if you made it."

Ana smiled and went back into the fridge. When she returned, she had two plates, each with a slice of what appeared to be a chocolate marmalade. I looked down at the dish and laughed.

Barry: "I was kidding about mud pies. So, what is this?"

Ana, laughing, said, "It's called chocolate dulce de batata. It's a jelly made from sweet potatoes."

I took a bite, savored it for a moment, and took another bite.

Barry: "Can I take back what I said about you being a chef? You're not a chef; you're an artist and food as your canvas. I've never tasted anything like this before."

Ana: "You are so sweet. I take pride in my cooking, and it's so nice it's appreciated."

I reached across the table and took her hand.

Barry: "Appreciation is not the word I would have used."

I felt her fingers tighten around my hand. Her fingers had an ever so slight tremble that suggested both fear and apprehension. Remembering my discussion with Lennon, the last thing I wanted her to feel was fear, so I let go of her hand and pulled my hand away, and took another bite of her batata. My actions seem to soothe her a bit. She smiled and said, "Let's finish our dessert and go into the living room to have some coffee."

Barry: "That sounds perfect. I have a million questions and want to know all about your life after we drifted apart."

Ana: "I'm an open book if you're interested."

We finished the dessert and Ana walked me to the living room. She turned on some background music and sat me down on a sofa across from a real wood fireplace burning. On the walls were pictures of Ana from all over the world, and in all of the photos, she was alone. She walked in with two cups of coffee, handed one to me, and sat down.

Ana: "I apologize for not asking you what you wanted in your coffee, but that's because this coffee is only made one way. It's an Indonesian coffee drink called kopi tubruk. I hope you enjoy it."

I took a sip and said, "It has a very unique flavor, but really good."

Ana: "I admit I added some brandy to it. That's not how it is made in Indonesia, but I figured it suited the moment."

I took another sip and put the coffee down and let my eyes wander around the room, looking at all the photos.

Barry: "You traveled to quite a lot of places, but I don't see anyone else in the photos. Did you have someone special to share all this with or did you travel alone?"

Ana: "I wasn't alone. My companion was my apron. Cooking was always my true love and I never felt lonely as long as I was cooking. That's why God allows me to cook for people here. It was Mr. Ponzi that suggested to God I be allowed to cook here, but when I was on Earth, no man ever equaled the feeling I got from cooking."

She paused for a moment to think and said, "That's not true. There was one man. I met him a long time ago, but fear drove me away from him. After that, I never met another man who made me feel the way he did. What about you? Was there ever someone?"

Barry: "There probably could have been, but I spent more energy finding what was wrong with my relationships than looking for what was right. I guess what bothered me most was that women were always trying to change me. I found myself wondering, why even go out with me if you feel the need to change me? They'd say they loved how I was confident and secure in my skin, but then they would spend the entire relationship trying to mold me into something that wasn't or would ever be me."

I paused for a moment to think.

Barry: "That sounds more like an excuse than a reason. I think the real reason I never found anyone was also fear. As John Lennon said to me, I wanted to be loved, but I was afraid of giving love. Afraid I would get hurt. I was hurt once and never wanted to experience that feeling again. For some strange reason, I'm no longer afraid. In fact, I don't think I'm afraid of anything anymore."

Ana: "I guess men and women are not as different as we think. We both have many of the same fears. They say men fear smart women, but women fear wise men too. They both feel vulnerable and do what they can, to bring a wise person down to their level, instead of aspiring to rise to his or her level. I used to be that way, but I figured out that another person's wisdom only made me better. So, now I embrace it. Speaking of wisdom, I remember you were always very smart, but now your wisdom seems to have replaced your smarts. And after reading your memoirs, I can see you have wisdom like no one I've ever known. How did that happen and why did you become a barber?"

Barry: "I don't know how wise I am, but if my wisdom has grown, I would have to give the credit to (or blame it on) the men whose hair I cut. I stumbled into being a barber and in a very short time, realized how much could be learned from standing behind that chair. I'm not sure why they bothered with me, but if I'm the wiser by it, I'm happy."

Ana: "Then you should be very happy."

I laughed, but the fact was, I had never been happier than I was at that moment, and it had nothing to do with that chair. We continued to talk, losing ourselves in conversation. We talk about our lives on Earth and where we wanted to be in this Heaven. Just when it seemed we had run out of things to talk about, the song "If You Don't Know Me by Now" by the Blue Notes came on the stereo.

Ana: "Remember this song?"

Barry: "How could I forget it?"

The truth was that for years, I couldn't stand listening to it because it reminded me of her, but at this moment, it was the perfect song. I stood up, held out my hand, and asked her to dance. She smiled, reminding me that the last time we heard this song together, she had asked me to dance. She took my hand and stood up. I put my arm around her waist as she put her arm over my shoulder. I noticed she wasn't trembling anymore. She put her head against my chest and a sensation came over me like I had never felt before. Was this what God intended? We danced, hardly moving our feet. As we danced, I could feel her fingers stroking the hair on the back of my neck. Everything was perfect. The song, the crackling of the fire, and the smell of her hair made it all feel like home.

My curiosity got the best of me, and I whispered in her ear, "So, what was so different about that one guy that set the bar so high?"

Without moving her head, she whispered back, "You truly are a very wise man, Barry, but sometimes you can be a bit slow. That guy was you." She stopped dancing and looked up at me.

I brushed her hair from her face and kissed her just as the chorus began. I pulled back, only to find her smiling as she moved forward to kiss me back. Her lips were so soft, so sweet. If I was to ever write about that moment, I didn't know if I could find the words. Maybe God was right. Sex wasn't as important as I thought because no sex, I ever had, equaled this feeling.

The song ended, but we kept dancing. The music became the crackling of the logs burning. Then something happened that was the last thing I ever expected. I thought, how could this be happening? If what Ana had told me about sex was true, why was I feeling this? I went to pull away, embarrassed, but she wouldn't let me. She held me tight, looked up at me, and said, "It's all right" and kissed me again.

This time, her kiss was laced with passion, and I couldn't help but return the passion as she pulled me into the bedroom.

Chapter XIV

Since there were no clocks in Heaven, there was no way to know how long we had laid in bed without speaking. I wondered to myself, had we done the wrong thing? It seemed like the right thing to do at the time, but would God agree, would He be angry and punish us, or worse… Then it came to mind that Ana was the only person that had told me there was no sex in Heaven. Everyone else I spoke to had an opinion but didn't seem to know for sure. Could she be wrong? I sure hoped she was. Things had been going so well here, and I would hate it if I had let everyone, especially God, down. I looked over at Ana.

Barry: "Tell me what you're thinking?"

Ana: "Oh, I feel a bit like Eve."

Barry: "Eve? As in Adam and Eve? Why would you feel like her?"

Ana: "Well, Eve seduced Adam with the apple. It appears I seduced you with my locro."

Laughing I said, "Oh, trust me, you might have tricked me into eating from the locro tree of knowledge but don't worry, I live to eat from all trees of knowledge. If there's one thing I've learned since coming to Heaven, it's that knowledge is one of God's proudest gifts to man and is the last thing He considers evil."

She smiled sweetly, kissed me softly, rolled to her side, and pushed her naked body up next to mine. We lay there for a few more minutes when there was a knock at her front door. We both leaped out of bed like guilty children and put our clothes on in record time. Ana went to the door and I could hear her speaking to someone. She came back with a puzzled look on her face.

Ana: "There's a guy at the door that says he needs a haircut. He apologized for interrupting but said Peter told him he could find you here. I asked him his name and he said, 'Jesus.'"

Barry: "The Jesus? As in Jesus Christ?"

Ana: "I've never seen him, so I don't know. Besides, he keeps looking down at the ground. He's very timid, but if it's him, you just moved up several notches on my totem pole of cool. I think you better go talk to him."

I scattered about to make myself look presentable and walked out to the door.

Jesus: "You must be Barry. My name is Jesus and I was told by Peter and my Father that I should come and get a haircut from you."

Barry: "It would be an honor to cut your hair. Shall we walk back to the shop?"

Jesus nodded, and we began to walk. He wasn't at all like I thought he'd be. He was a man of color, but not exceptionally handsome whose hair and beard appeared to have been neglected for quite a while. His voice was soft and like Ana said, very timid. On our walk back to the shop, he never said a word, looking down at the ground the whole way. When we got into the shop, I motioned for him to have a seat, which he did, surveying every move with extreme caution. Once he was relatively comfortable, I asked him how he wanted his hair cut.

Jesus: "My Father said I should clean up my hair and beard so I look more presentable."

There seemed to be a pattern emerging. "My Father said... My Father told me." Always spoken with a submissive timbre in his voice. He sat there, with his shoulders slightly rolled forward, not saying a word, but not like he was in deep thought. In fact, he seemed to be in some sort of a vacuum-like mental black hole. I thought I must be reading this wrong. This was Jesus Christ, the Son of God, but at the same time, he was reminiscent of many children who had come into my shop on Earth with one of their parents. I would ask the parent how I should cut the child's hair and they would say, "Whatever he wants," but when I asked the child and he told me what he wanted, the parent would interrupt, "Oh, you don't want that. You won't look good with that haircut. You should cut it this way." I would see the expression on the child's face immediately change and he would look exactly like Jesus did.

Barry: "Is that what you really want me to do? It seems like you want a different haircut. You can tell me what you want. I mean, you're Jesus. I will do whatever you want me to do."

Jesus: "Well, I guess what I would like is a haircut like you gave Lucifer. I'm tired of looking like Jesus Christ. It sucks being the Son of God. Everyone recognizes you wherever you go and all I ever get when people come up to me is, 'Hi, Jesus, how's your Father?' No one ever asks me how I'm doing. I would love to be able to walk around Heaven without being recognized."

Barry: "Then a fade haircut, it is."

I thought that might bring a smile to his face, but instead, he got very fidgety. I reached for the clipper, put on the attachment, and was about to begin when he stopped me.

Jesus: "Wait! Maybe I shouldn't. Do you think my Father will like it?"

Barry: "You would know better than me. I've never met Him. And even if He doesn't like it, it's your hair…right?"

Jesus: "Yes, but I'm not very good at conflict. Especially with my Father."

Barry: "If I remember right, you seemed more than capable of dealing with conflict at that temple court, knocking over tables and accusing the merchants of being a bunch of thieves and robbers."

Jesus: "Oy, and I never heard the end of that from my Father. All I heard after that was, 'I didn't send you to Earth to start a fight. You're supposed to be the Prince of Peace and instead, you acted like a raging bull.' The truth is, He never stood by me when I was on there. He either told me what to do or criticized me for everything I did. I felt like I was always walking on eggshells. If it wasn't for Lucifer, I don't know if I could have gotten through it. Luc kept me grounded and helped me through some very rough times. It's a known fact that my Father was not happy with my performance on Earth and found little to praise me for. He seems to have all the patience in the world for humans and angels, but little, if any, for me."

Barry: "I understand what you're saying. My father was the same way. Of course, my father wasn't God. The good news is, when I finally stood up for myself, his anger turned to respect."

Jesus: "Yeah, but your father couldn't snap his fingers and make you disappear. I was expected to always toe the line on Earth.. no wiggle room. If it wasn't His idea, it was a bad idea. I didn't have a choice. and no free will. He always talks about His love of free will with everyone except me. With me, it was His way or the highway…or worse."

Barry: "I really do understand in my own insignificant way. My father wasn't God; he was just a school teacher and like yours, I saw the patience he had for his students, but when it came to me, if I didn't get it right the first time, I was a hopeless cause. As I got older, I realized it was my fault for letting him treat me like that. The moment I stood up for myself, it all changed."

Our discussion seemed to open him up a bit and I began to understand the reason for his timidness. All he wanted was his Father's approval and support. I knew that feeling and maybe if he showed he was not afraid to make his own decisions, he might get that approval he wanted so badly. So, I took a bold approach.

Barry: "I think a fade, like Luc's, would look great on you. Let's do it!"

He smiled for the first time and said, " Yeah, let's do it, and if my Father doesn't like it, I'll blame it on you."

I laughed, but my laugh lacked enthusiasm. I thought to myself, What have I gotten myself into? What if God didn't like the haircut? What if I was wrong about standing up to Him? Even worse, what if it pissed Him off? I guess it was too late to concern myself with that, so I grabbed my clippers and began to cut the fade up the side of his head.

Barry: "You said your Father wasn't happy with your performance on Earth? It seems to me that you did pretty darn good. After all, there are more Christians today than any other religion in the world, and you're responsible for that."

Jesus: "Most of them aren't Christians. They use me to validate their own self-interests. I told them to help the poor and needy, to love their enemies, and to put everyone above themselves, but did they listen? No, they enslaved humans, murder millions of innocent people in wars, and would rather throw food away before ever giving it to the millions starving. They are destroying their planet in the name of gold while complaining that the money in their pocket belongs to them and no one else. That's not what I preached."

Barry: "Well, you don't seem to be holding back your anger right now."

Jesus: "No, I'm not. I'm pissed off. My message was crystal clear and they ignored it. And don't get me started on the disciples. I was up on that damn Cross, with my hands nailed to it, and what did they do to help me? Cowards, the lot of them."

Barry: "You sound bitter."

Jesus: "I'm not bitter, just pissed. This has been stewing inside me for a millennium and if my Father ever asked me to return to Earth, I would refuse. I don't care what He does to me. Humans just don't get it. The reason for me being there was not for them to worship me, but to live by the message I brought them from my Father. Their Bible claims I said I am God, worship me but in the next breath, it says there is only one God. My Father is the only God; I'm not God and I never said I was. You don't have to be a mathematician to understand that one means one. But what can you expect? My Father abandoned them with only their free will to guide them. Leave a child to make the rules and guess what you get? Childish rules! Give me a break! If I was God, anyone that wrote that rubbish they call the Bible would not step foot in Heaven."

Barry: "Have you told Him this? Maybe you should."

Jesus: "You might be right. One thing I learned on Earth was, if I don't stand up for myself, who will? Certainly not my Father. After all He did before I went to Earth, where was He when I was there? Where were my ten plagues or my Genesis flood? He left me hanging on that Cross and didn't lift a finger."

Barry: "Since I'm not a scholar of the Bible, I don't think it's my place to speak to any of this, but didn't you die to forgive the sins of man? I mean, that seems to be a noble cause."

That only seem to feed his anger as he slammed his hand on the arm of his mid-century chair.

Jesus: "I died because the Romans nailed me to a cross, jammed a spear in me and no one did anything to stop them. The whole died to forgive their sins is disciple crap. There was no reason for me to die. It was just man's free will and that's how they twisted it to make it all right. Well, it wasn't all right. And because of my Father's love of man's free will, He didn't lift a finger to help me. Maybe if dear ol' Dad had been given me more time and a few more miracles, everything might have been different Moses led the Israelites for forty years across a desert and lived to be a hundred and twenty years old to spread his message. He gave Noah one hundred and twenty years to build the ark and gather the animals. I began to convert the whole world to Christianity at the age of thirty and He gave me just three years to spread The Word? Three lousy years! I barely got my message out in Israel, let alone the whole world. How was I supposed to spread it throughout the world in that short amount of time? Even my resurrection was only witnessed by a handful of people. I don't mean to cast aspersions on Him, but that failure was not on me, it was completely His fault."

All of a sudden, this timid young man had become full of rage and anger. I didn't want to promote it anymore and worried that I might have been responsible for letting an angry genie out of the bottle. I wasn't sure how to change the direction of this conversation, but I did my best.

Barry: "So what do you do to pass your time here in Heaven?"

As silly as it was, my question seemed to calm him for the moment.

Jesus: "Not much. Mary Magdalene and I are kinda homebodies. Being who I am, it's hard for me to go anywhere without getting mobbed. Most are respectful, but it gets tiresome. So, we just stay at home. Sometimes we just cuddle up on the sofa and watch a TV show. Boy, do I wish there was TV when

I was on Earth. It would have really helped to get the message out. After all, an hour doesn't pass that some idiot isn't on TV, preaching his word and calling it my Word, while all the time, filling his pockets with gold."

Suddenly, a light went on in my head. Who would know more about what's in God's mind than His son? Maybe he could answer my most pressing question.

Barry: "If you don't mind, you could help me to understand something."

Jesus: "I'd be happy to help if I can."

Barry: "It's a personal question, and I won't be offended if you tell me it's none of my business, but please, understand I have a good reason for asking."

Jesus: "I'm an open book."

He chuckled and said, "I have no choice, I'm the Son of God."

I hesitated for a moment, then asked, "Do you and Mary ever have sex? I asked because I have met someone that I have deep feelings for and I've been told there is no sex in Heaven."

Jesus broke out laughing. "Is that all? Yeah, we have sex, and I can honestly say, she's really good at it. Is that special person the lovely lady that answered the door?"

Barry: "Yeah, that's her. Something happened a while ago and I have been so worried that we had broken Heaven's rules and that God might be disappointed in us. So, tell me, why doesn't anyone know there's sex here?"

He laughed even louder.

Jesus: "Well, it's fairly new here in Heaven. My Father figured out that He dropped the ball on that fine line between love, passion, and lust. He decided the solution was to get rid of lust, so now we have no interest in sex unless there's a deep connection between two people. The reason you don't hear about it is that everyone that has sex feels the same way you do. They think they've done something wrong and keep it to themselves outta fear. But my Father knows all and laughs a lot that they think they are hiding it. If there is just one thing I can teach you about Heaven, it's that there are no secrets here. My Father knows everything that goes on here and many times, it's His doing."

Barry: "So, it's the best unkept secret in Heaven. Well, for me, it's a great relief. So, how did you meet Mary?"

Jesus: "Lucifer introduced us. I owe him so much. I don't know how I can ever repay him. He has saved my butt more times than I can remember. He's truly a great friend and an even greater angel."

Barry: "I cut his hair earlier and liked him a lot, but I have to admit, I was a bit intimidated. I couldn't stop thinking he was the Prince of Darkness."

Jesus: "That's funny. Did he pull that 'lay your soul to waste' crap on you? The truth is, he's a pussy cat. He wouldn't hurt a fly. He serves my Father as a voice of reason and only cares about helping people to become the best they can be. Of course, as they always do, man needed someone to blame for their shortcomings and Luc was the perfect scapegoat. Who better to blame than the angel that made a joke that my Father didn't think was funny and sent packing? What's hilarious is that if he told my Father that same joke today, He would probably laugh."

Barry: "Well, to say this conversation has been enlightening would be an understatement."

I finished his haircut and decided to keep his beard long and blended it into the fade. I turned him toward the mirror to give him the first look at his new do and asked him what he thought.

Jesus: "I love it! Exactly what I wanted. Now I can walk home and no one will recognize me. Not to mention, Mary will be happy for many reasons. First and foremost, that I did what I wanted, instead of always doing what my Father told me to do. She never lets me forget that it's my life and gets mad at me every time I back down to my Father."

He snickered like a teenager and said, "Boy, am I

gonna get some when I get home."

Barry: "I hope your Father likes it too."

Jesus: "I hope He does, but if He doesn't, fuck it. I love it and I know Mary will too. That's all that matters! Thank you so much for bringing out what's been inside for so long. I feel liberated."

I removed the cloth, brushed him off, and he got up, but this time with his shoulders back and his head up.

Jesus: "If I had any friends, I would recommend they come for a haircut. Maybe now I will make new friends and they will like me for who I am, not what I am. I have you to thank for that."

Who I am, not what I am seemed to be a common thread amongst the very famous. There was something so very lonely about them, and I felt sorry that none of them had friends, so I asked him, "Maybe you and Mary can join us for dinner one night. Ana is an amazing cook and is always excited to cook for people. You know, just before I left with you, she told me that if it was you, I would move up several notches on her totem pole of cool. If you and Mary came over for dinner, I think I would go straight to the top of that pole and you wouldn't be the only one getting some."

Jesus: "That would be great. We haven't eaten in so long. I'm sure Mary would love it. She does get lonely with no real friends and it would be nice to make some. Can I invite Luc too?"

Barry: "Of course, but please, tell him not to scare Ana. We don't want her looking over her shoulder while she's cooking."

Chapter XV

I couldn't wait to tell Ana about my talk with Jesus and what he said about sex, but first, I had to clean up a mountain of hair and write in my notebook. It seemed to me that the more haircuts I did, the better my writing got. I had already written twice what Gerty had asked for and was anxious to hear what she thought. Not that it mattered anymore. I was feeling really good about it and nothing negative she might say could change that, although a little constructive criticism couldn't hurt.

I finished writing and sat back in the chair to reflect on all that I had experienced so far in Heaven. Who could ever imagine a simple barber like me would ever cut the hair of such an eclectic group of great minds? I was just about to get up and go to Ana's when I spied a cowboy peeping through the window. He was of average height and weight, with a Western bow tie and his hat tipped back on his head. He motioned to me if he could come in and get a haircut. I didn't recognize him, but that had become quite common here, so I motioned him in.

He walked in, took off his hat, scratched the back of his head, and said, "My hair has been ticklin' my ears and saw your window. I figure if you're good enough for God, you are surely good enough for me.

I asked him his name and he said his friends called him Billy.

Barry: "I'm Barry. It's very nice to meet you, Billy. How would you like your hair cut?"

Billy, looking down while scratching his head: "Well, I'll tell you, Barry. This haircut has served me well throughout my life, so I would be much appreciative if you could duplicate it."

It was one of the worst haircuts I'd ever seen. Skeetched up the sides to the skin, with long hair on the top, and the two weren't even blended, but if that was what he wanted, that was what he would get. I wrapped him up, pulled out the clippers, and started in.

Barry: "So, Billy, what do you do to pass the time in Heaven?"

Billy: "Well, since I'm nothing more than an old cowpuncher, I spend most of my time practicing my lariat tricks."

Barry: "Are there cows in Heaven, or do you practice on humans?

Billy: "Is there a difference? Humans are as fearful as cows. You know, if you stomped your foot behind a bobcat, he would turn with claws out to protect itself from whatever danger lie behind him. Do the same to a cow or a human and they'll stampede in the other direction. Humans, with all the advantages God has blessed them with, seem content to react in the same way as the lessor creatures in His Grand Design. They might very well be God's greatest failure. In fact, after seeing what we've become, it wouldn't surprise me if God decided to sue us for calling Him our Father"

There was something contagious about his smile and delivery. I believed he could make a weather report funny. I found myself laughing at everything he said. As he spoke, for a moment, I was laughing so hard that I was afraid the clipper would slip out of my hand.

Barry: "You're a very funny man, Billy. Did people consider you a comedian when you lived on Earth?"

Billy: "Some said I was, but to be honest, I don't

tell jokes. I just watch man and report the facts. What I enjoyed the most was talking about the one thing man claims to relish more than anything else but ignores when it comes to his everyday life: his common sense. Seems to me, whether it is here in Heaven or back on Earth, common sense ain't that common. Although I must admit, that's even more true on Earth. On Earth, there are three kinds of men. A handful who learn by readin', a few who learn by observing, and the rest have to pee on an electric fence for themselves. I guess I'm one of those few who observe because I'm not the best reader and I've never learned much from peeing on a fence."

My stomach hurt from laughing and I understood why his haircut was so bad. Who could cut hair while laughing this hard? What made it even funnier was that he wasn't trying to be funny. He was a true master of the art of subtlety. Something I had aspired to be my whole life.

Barry: "You know, Billy, I have cut hair for some of the greatest thinkers the world has ever known, yet I find myself listening to you with the greatest interest. I have always believed that humor cuts through the muck of facts and opinions. You are truly a great humorist."

Billy scratched his head again like he was looking for something to say.

Billy: "Well, there's no trick to being a humorist when you have the whole world working for you. Man, with all his bluster and delusions of grandeur, is his own greatest obstacle to the greatness God had intended for him. I use to think government, not man, was the problem, but since I arrived here, in Heaven, and look back on Earth, I realize the government was just a symptom. Man created government so he would have someone to blame for all his mistakes and shortcomings. Man is like the dog that buries a bone and blames the field when he forgets where he buried it."

Barry: "So, you no longer criticize the government for the ills of man?"

Billy: "Oh, don't get me wrong. Most countries seem to run despite their government, not because of it, but government is nothing more than man's scapegoat that quenches his thirst to be the victim rather than the problem. And as someone once told me, it's easier to play the victim, because the victim doesn't have to change himself."

Laughing, I said, "So, when you're not practicing your lariat tricks, what do you do here in Heaven?"

Billy: "I guess you could say, I'm an advisor to God, although, I don't know if He has ever taken any of my advice."

Barry: "So, what is your most recent advice?"

Billy: "To rid man of his pride, envy, and selfishness."

Barry: "Well, I don't see how He could argue with that. So, what did you say?"

Billy: "I told Him that although I know they weren't in His plan originally, they are a byproduct of a person's need to feel important and the biggest obstacle to the success of their free will. It seems to me that somewhere along the way, man lost his way. This thirst to be important made humans forget that a life lived for others is a life worthwhile. Then again, maybe that was never true except for a handful of people. For most of us, this thirst to possess is the same as the camel in the Sahara has for water. We think the more possessions we have, the more important we are, but the truth is, you can only drink so much water.

It used to be that if you wanted to be successful, all you had to do was know what you're doing, love what you're doing, and believe in what you're doing. That was the formula for most of the great entrepreneurs, understanding that the money would follow. Now it's if you didn't die rich, you died a failure. Mr. Carnegie said it best when he said the man who dies rich, dies disgraced, but today he'd be laughed out of the room. Entrepreneurs like him have been eaten alive by the businessmen, and selfishness has gotten so bad that Mr. Webster is threatening to remove the word selfless from his dictionary. Don't get me wrong, I never had a problem with men becoming wealthy; it's how they become wealthy and what they did with their wealth. It's not very hard to conclude that man no longer worships God but rather his own pocketbook."

Barry: "Is selfishness God's fault? Did His Grand Plan miss that?"

Billy: "Well, to some degree, yes. He gave man the precious power of free will. I relish that as much as any other man, but as with everything, it comes with responsibility and the understanding that a person's actions can either serve himself or mankind. It is his choice and sadly, most decide out of fear, greed, and loathing, to choose themselves. That wasn't God's intention, but rather than benefitting from this great gift of free will, they have allowed themselves to become victims of it. What's even sadder is that many who are not rich support the rich for the simple reason that they think they will be rich one day. And that's nothing more than a fool's dream."

Barry: "A lot of people who have sat in that chair have questioned God's obsession with free will, including Jesus. Did you ever advise Him on free will?"

Billy: "I told Him if you ride a horse bridle-free, chances are, the rider will never reach his destination. As long as you allow the horse to go its own way, you will most likely never wind up in the right place."

Barry: "Well, for a simple cowpoke who rounds up dogies, your lasso landed perfectly around that neck. I can understand why God asks for your advice and I can't imagine Him not taking it. Since I got here, I've cut the hair of a lot of very famous people. All of them had great advice and here I am cutting the hair of a scruffy simple man who, quite honestly, has one of the worst haircuts I have ever seen, and he makes more sense than all those experts."

Billy: "Well, as I said, it is not common practice for humans to use their common sense. I'm no different from anyone else, except I take the time to think about stuff. Most people don't like to think. I don't know why. Maybe it hurts, but they seem to feel comfortable letting others think for them. And when they do think, they think only as far as necessary to support what notions they already have. Ask them to go one step further, and they'll instantly stop thinking and become a rodent on the edge of a precipice following those in front. A perfect condition for religion."

Barry: "What do you mean?"

Billy: "Man, by his actions, is the laziest of all animals. God gave mankind the ability to make things better, but sadly, he has only used it to make things easier. Knowing this, many of man's 'religious' leaders cherry-pick God's word and use it as the shortest route to their own personal gains, knowing their followers will simply shake their heads up and down. The fact of the matter is that God never intended them to shake their heads at all. His grand plan was that free will should always end with a question mark."

Barry: "So, shouldn't God be addressing those leaders, rather than man as a whole?"

Billy: "I'm not saying the leaders shouldn't be judged by our Heavenly Father, but man has no one to blame but himself. I remember once running into a friend on the street. I asked him how his day was going and he told me it was horrible. He explained that he had bought a horse from a local horse trader and it went lame a couple of miles from the stable. I asked where he was going now, and he said back to the horse trader to buy another horse. It was apparent to me that he, like the majority of man, was oblivious to the obvious."

Barry: "So, what did you suggest God do about man's reluctance to do the right thing?"

Billy: "Well, I think like an ol' cowpoke, so I suggested He tighten the lariat. Send a sheriff to Earth to perform a couple of celestial lariat tricks, and when man becomes mesmerized, hogtie him and burn a new brand just above his flank."

Barry: "Sounds like a good plan. What did He say?"

Billy: "He didn't say anything. He never does, and I don't expect Him to. After all, I'm just a simple cowboy and He's God. It would be presumptuous of me to think I knew more on anything than Him."

Barry: "But if He isn't going to take your advice, why did He ask for your opinion? I'm just a barber, but my common sense tells me that there are some things really wrong with the way things are. It may not be His fault, but does that mean they should be ignored?"

Billy: "I don't think He's ignoring it. In fact, I think He listens to every word I say. He has tough decisions to make to find a balance. It's not easy to find that right balance, and I sure don't know what it is. I remember being in a stampede years ago. We all know that a stampede is a bad thing, but if the cattle are going in the right direction, it makes the job easier for the cowpoke. He understands that and is reluctant to herd man like cattle. He'd rather let them stampede in the hope that it will be in the right direction."

Barry: "I don't know much about cattle drives, but if you ask me, man is already stampeding in the wrong direction. You said it yourself. Mankind has lost its purpose and seems to have lost its way. They need a new cowpoke to herd them back in the right direction, and although I don't claim to have the answers, I think God needs to step up and give that cowpoke a road map."

Billy: "I think He knows that, but He's trying to find the best voice. When He finds that voice, He will send him back to Earth to spread the word."

Barry: "Well, according to Jesus, it isn't going to be him next time. He made a pretty good case that he wasn't given a chance to spread the word and wants nothing to do with it."

Billy: "I think he's right. I think his Father realized that the conditions in those days weren't suitable to get the word out. Walking from town to town is not conducive to world enlightenment. Maybe that's why He shortened his stay on Earth. But today, man's technology has made the world a tiny place, and it is much easier to get His word out. Today, they have this thing I heard about called going viral. It is a powerful tool that can help spread His word. That is if the right person is spreading it. The problem is that no one, including God, really understands what makes something go viral"

Barry: "I'm impressed that you know about going viral and you're right, no one can really explain why something goes viral. It's almost magical. But even if God is successful in getting his message viral, the biggest obstacle is to prevent that voice from being drowned out by the crazies and the manipulators. How can His messenger separate himself from them?"

Billy: "Humor! People take their comedians seriously and their leaders as a joke. If that person can make people laugh at the charlatans, he wins. That's why Jesus isn't the best choice. He's not funny at all."

Barry: "I noticed that, but if you're right, you might be the perfect person. Has He asked you?"

Billy: "No, but that's because He knows I have no interest in putting myself out there to be examined with a spyglass. I'm quite proud of my shortcomings and smart enough to know better than to sell my parrot to the town gossip."

Just then, Billy looked over at the table where my notebook was. He reached over and picked it up.

Billy: "What's this?"

Barry: "Oh, it's something I've been writing since I got here. I just wanted to chronicle my new life."

Billy: "Can I read a little of it?"

Barry: "If you want. I don't know how good it is, but I sure do enjoy writing it."

Billy began to turn through the pages, stopping

now and then to scratch his head and laugh. I tried to say something once, and he held his hand up to stop me from talking and went back to reading. So, I decided that while he read, I would try to put the finishing touches on his haircut around his scratching and laughing. When I finished, I stood back and looked at it, realizing it just might be the best Billy's hair has ever looked. I was about to ask him what he thought when he surprised me with a question.

Billy: "Judging by what I just read, you seem to be a pretty smart cattle herder yourself and an above-average humorist. Have you ever thought about volunteering to be the person to go back to Earth?"

Barry: "I'm flattered that you would think that, but why would anyone listen to me? I'm a nobody, a barber from West Los Angeles."

Billy laughed and said, "Why would they listen to me? You suggested I should go back to Earth and be God's messenger. I'm nothing but a cowboy with a lariat."

Barry: "But you're much more than that. You're funny, smart, and most important, as wise as anyone I ever met. I'm just a barber that likes to write his stories and probably not very good at it."

Billy: "Oh, you're good at it. Just reading the few pages I read, one can see that, but I already knew you're more than just a barber. You have a talent I could never have. You bring people out. I came here to get a haircut. Nothing more, but after just a few minutes, I not only felt safe to tell you anything, but I felt excited to tell you. You also challenged me to think by asking questions. Good questions. You see, most people tell, but you ask and you ask in a way that makes it simple for a person to find the answer. That's a rare talent and maybe more important than humor."

I had never been very good at receiving compliments and usually dismiss them quickly with a self-deprecating joke. So, rather than discussing it more, I simply thanked him and turned him toward the mirror, and asked if he liked the haircut.

Billy: "Looks better than this ol' face deserves. I came in looking like something that would make a freight train take a dirt road, and I'm leaving with a newfound understanding of what a handsome man faces when walking down the street. A welcomed risk that I'm more than willing to take."

Barry: "Well, I'm glad you like it. By the way, what's your last name, Billy?"

Billy: "Rogers."

Barry: "Wait...Rogers? You're Will Rogers? The Will Rogers?"

Billy scratched his head again and said, "Yep.

Guilty as charged."

I removed the cloth and brushed him off and again wondered to myself, What the hell is going on and what is God up to? There had to be some reason all these famous intellectuals had come in for haircuts. All this wasn't just a coincidence. There had to be more to it, but what was it and how did I fit in? I wondered if Will knew or was he just a pawn in all this. So, I asked one last question.

Barry: "Hey, Will, do you think God has some special plan for me?"

Billy: "It's not my place to say, Barry. Only He knows that. I will tell you one thing, but I'll deny having ever told you."

Barry: "What's that?"

He motioned me to come close and whispered in my ear, "People don't get haircuts in Heaven."

He sat back smiling that infectious smile, thanked me for the haircut, got up, and started walking out. When he reached the door, he stopped, scratched his head again, put his hat on with the front of it pointed toward the sky, and walked out twirling his lariat.

Chapter XVI

P*eople don't get haircuts in Heaven?* What did Will mean, *people don't get haircuts in Heaven?* How was I supposed to react to that? I sure didn't need cutting hair as a gift from God, like Ana's cooking. There was little doubt in my mind that this was a devious plot, but for what purpose? I had just finished writing about my experience with Will when the front door opened in walked Luc.

Luc: "Got a couple of minutes to clean me up?"

After what Will told me, I wasn't about to trust anyone, especially Luc, but I decided to play along to see where this might be heading.

Barry: "Grew awfully fast, didn't it? In all the years I have been cutting hair, I've never seen hair grow that fast. Maybe that's because you're an angel, not human."

Luc: "Yeah, maybe, but look at it. It's all grown out. The fade is gone."

He sat down in anticipation of me draping him up, but I had no intention of doing that until I got an explanation of what the hell was going on.

Barry: "A funny thing just happened, Luc. Some guy, whose hair I was cutting, just told me that people don't get haircuts in Heaven. Sounds crazy, huh?"

I waited for a moment to see Luc's reaction. He looked like a dog with its tail between its legs.

Barry: "Is that true Luc?"

Luc: "Who told you that?"

Barry: "It doesn't matter. Is it true?"

Luc: "Does that matter? I mean, have you suffered from it?"

Barry: "Yeah, it matters. All of you and God tricked me and I don't like being tricked."

Luc: "It was never anyone's intention to trick you, especially God. His reasons were to inspire, educate, and motivate you. And judging by your notebook, it worked."

Barry: "How do you know about my notebook? I didn't even have it when I cut your hair. So, tell me, Luc, at this point, why should I believe a word you say?"

Luc: "Barry, this isn't Earth; it's Heaven. Man may control his destiny on Earth, but God rules Heaven, and please don't question His motives."

Barry: "Well, I am. I'm questioning everything here in Heaven. Didn't you tell Gerty I was a curious man that relishes the question? Well, I'm questioning."

Luc: "I'm not suggesting you don't question what's going on, but take some advice and don't question His motives. That is a recipe for disaster. I questioned His motives once and look where it got me. I understand you're angry and confused, but trust me on this one thing, it will all become clear very soon."

Barry: "And why should I trust you? More importantly, why should I continue cutting hair? I'd rather be spending my time with Ana, or is she just another pawn in this grand practical joke?"

Luc: "It's not a practical joke, and Ana's feelings for you are real. In fact, I don't think God ever anticipated your feelings for each other being so deep, so fast. I know right now, you don't trust me, but you have something very special with Ana. Don't blow it with question marks."

Barry: "My whole existence here right now is one big question mark. How can I trust her or anyone else?"

Luc: "I understand why you feel that way, and I certainly don't expect you to trust me or God at this point, but trust your heart and look into Ana's eyes. She adores you. So, do yourself a favor and cherish every breath you take when you're with her."

Just then, the door opened, and in walked Gerty. Without a word, she went straight to my notebook, sat down, and began reading. I ignored it because what she thought of my writing was the last thing I cared about at that moment and continued my war of words with Luc.

Barry: "Seems to me that if God has to trick someone, like me, into doing something, he's not the perfect God we all think he is."

Luc: "Of course He's not perfect, and He'd be the first one to tell you. If He was perfect, would there be wars, hunger, power, and greed on Earth? Only man puts Him on that pedestal. He's learning on the fly, but He is in charge and the only chance any of us have is with Him. Look at it like Heaven and Earth is a video game and God's the programmer. No video game is perfect. The programmer continually works to make it better and better. Consider all this as Creation 2.0."

Barry: "So, do you know where all this is going?"

Luc: "I expect you won't believe me, but no. Like everyone else you've met, I'm merely a player in this game. If I knew, I would tell you. What I will tell you is to roll with the flow. I'm confident that your questions will all be answered at some point down the road."

Damn, Luc is good! I was ready to throw this whole thing into a dumpster and call it quits. Now, my anger had turned to curiosity. Just then, Gerty burst out like she hadn't heard a word we had said (which was probably true).

Gerty: "This is good. You've gotten better in every chapter, but you are missing one thing."

I was worn out from arguing with Luc and I knew there was no ignoring Gerty.

Barry apathetically: "What am I missing, Gerty?"

Gerty: "You are writing with the pen of an apprentice. To be a successful writer, you must become a master. You have gained all this knowledge, now what are you going to do with it?"

I was tired from arguing and had little energy left to confront her. Besides, I knew she was right. It was time to become a master. If I was to ever expect anyone to read what I wrote, I would have to be unique and not just a parrot.

Luc: "Can you see him becoming a master, Gerty?"

Gerty: "If what my friend Sam Clemens told me is true, the answer is yes. He just has to stand up and speak louder in his own voice. Of course, that's easier said than done, but it's possible."

Barry: "What do you mean by speaking louder in my own voice?"

Gerty: "You've done a marvelous job of reporting. Now it's time to take it to the next level. Don't be satisfied with others' opinions. Come up with your own and don't be afraid of them being heard. Certainly, none of the others are always right. Be brave and use all you have received here and personalize it. No one wants to read chronicles of someone else's voice; they want to hear your voice. Speak loudly and carry the stick of confidence."

Barry: "But those people are either famous or infamous. I'm a barber. Why would anyone care what a barber thinks?"

Luc: "What do you think made them famous? Do you think they were born famous? They worked hard to become who they are. John Lennon was an art student, Mark Twain was a steamboat pilot, and Will Rogers was the son of a cattle rancher who did lariat tricks. You're a barber about to become God's prophet."

Barry: "What the hell do you mean about to become God's prophet?"

Gerty: "Did you think all this was just a coincidence? You're smarter than that…isn't he, Luc?"

Luc: "God thinks so, and that's all that matters."

Barry: "What are you saying?"

Gerty: "God has been watching you for quite a while. He sees something, although, at this moment, I haven't a clue what it is."

Barry: "So, did He send all you guys to the shop?"

Gerty: "Of course He sent us. Do you think I would have bothered if He hadn't? I don't have the time or the interest in wasting my time musing a nobody."

Luc: "Oh shut the fuck up, Gerty. You're nothing more than another pawn in this whole thing, just like the rest of us. You did what God told you to do and you don't have a clue what His plan is."

Gerty: "You shut the fuck up. Where would he be without my help?"

Barry: "Both of you shut the fuck up. I have a thousand questions and I want answers. My first question…is Ana part of this grand plot?"

Luc: "Not at all. She's innocent and loves you very much."

Barry: "She loves me?"

Gerty: "Oh, please! You really can't tell?"

She looked over at Luc with a look of disgust on her face.

Gerty: "This is hopeless. He has no self-confidence and certainly has no insight. We're wasting our time."

Luc: "Well, you tell God. I sure the hell won't. I just got back to Heaven after questioning His Grand

Design and I have no intention of being thrown out again. Whether God thinks he's the new prophet or not, is no business of mine. I just do what he wants me to do and be happy he asked."

Barry: "I'm no prophet; I'm a barber!"

Luc: "Jesus was a carpenter before he became the Messiah."

Barry: "So, you're comparing me to him? You've got to be kidding."

Gerty: "If that's all you think of yourself, then a barber is all you'll ever be. I can bring the horse to water, but it's up to you to drink. You're standing at a precipice. You're good, now you have to decide whether you want to be great."

Luc: "I never thought I would hear myself say this, but Gerty is right. You have a special talent. God recognized it, I recognized it, but it's all meaningless if you don't recognize it."

Maybe I was just numb from all the emotions I was feeling right then, and despite feeling very betrayed, I had to admit that most of what the two of them were saying made sense. What didn't make sense was that it was me they were talking about. Had it been anyone else, I would be all on board, but how was I supposed to buy into this?

So, how do I respond to this? Do I laugh, do I get really scared, or do I accept it? At least, for now,

I can't accept it, so that leaves laugh or scared. But before I could decide, the front door opened again, and in came Ana looking drop-dead gorgeous.

Barry: "Ana, you look beautiful!"

She walked over to me, put her hands on my cheeks, smiled, and as soft as anyone could ever imagine, kissed me on the lips. She looked over and saw Lucifer and Gerty.

Ana: "I'm sorry, did I come at a bad time?"

I didn't want to say it out loud, but her timing couldn't be more perfect.

Barry: "Not at all. Let me introduce you to Gertrude Stein and Lucifer. Be careful if you shake his hand. He looks hungry and has a habit of biting people he claims to like on the ass."

Gerty: "It's a pleasure to meet you, young lady. One day soon, we are going to have to talk about this young man you are so much in love with."

Ana: "And what would you like to talk to me about regarding this young man I love?"

She loves me? Is that true, or is this more of the same deception? As much as I wanted to believe it, how could I? These revelations had left me with the inability to trust anything or anyone in Heaven. But I loved her, and I didn't want to risk losing her if she was sincere.

Luc: "It's a pleasure to meet you, Ana. I hope

you appreciate how very lucky a woman you are, to have someone like Barry love you as much as he does."

Ana looked over at me with a smile of pride and embarrassment.

Ana: "I do."

Luc: "Well, Gerty, I think we best go on our way. I hope you think about what we talked about, Barry."

Ana: "Can I ask, what were you talking about?"

Barry: "These fools think I'm a prophet for God. Imagine that, Ana, me, a prophet."

Gerty: "We didn't say you were a prophet, we said you could become one, but you have a long ways to go."

Ana: "So, Ms. Stein, what does he have to do to become this prophet?"

Gerty: "First, he has to believe he can. That's easier said than done. The best way to do it is to question the status quo. Those of us whose hair he cut are the status quo. He has to absorb everything we talked about and kick it up a notch. He can do it, but he needs to believe he can."

Barry: "And I keep asking why would anyone listen to a barber?"

Luc: "Remember how you felt about Will when you thought he was just a cowboy? You had no problem accepting what he said even though he was, in your mind, only a guy with a really bad haircut who did lariat tricks. People will accept you just like you accepted him if what you say makes sense and you say it undeniably. That is one of your strengths and you know it. Mix in a couple of miracles and bam!"

Barry: "Wait...how did you know about Will?"

The more I heard, the more I felt deceived and manipulated. What exactly did you two have to do with this?"

Luc: "I admit that God put Gerty and me in charge. We're guilty of putting this together, but it was never to deceive or manipulate you. It was to do two things. First, to find out if you have what it takes, and second, to prepare you to fulfill your destiny."

Barry: "Destiny? Exactly what is my destiny?"

Luc: "If I knew that, I would tell you. We're just the builders, God is the engineer. We don't know what it is we're building. Our job is to put one brick on another according to His design."

Barry: "Why do I feel like a two-by-four? I don't mean to tell you two what to do, but if you wanted me to learn from all those people and take that knowledge further, you should have considered creating some conflict between them. Or, in basketball terms, a little one-on-one."

Gerty: "He's right, Luc. How could we expect him to become wise by simply listening to these men of letters and science? Without interaction and conflict, he is nothing but a parrot and there's nothing special about being a parrot."

Barry: "I'm not suggesting that I'm even interested in becoming a prophet, because I'm not, but if I was interested, I would need to see all these mentors (for better or worse) bouncing their ideas off each other to find the common denominators and the conflicts."

Ana: "I know I'm an outsider here, but I have an idea. If you two could get all of these men to come to my house, I would love to cook for everyone and all of you could sit around my table discussing and debating and Barry could ask all the questions he needs to come to his own opinion."

Luc: "Barry, you may not be the wisest man I have ever met (yet), but you are the luckiest to have such a wise woman on your side. Ana, that's a brilliant idea."

Barry: "Ana, I love you, but I have to ask. Was that your idea or is it just more of God's bullshit?"

Ana: "I would never lie to you, sweetheart; it was suggested by someone who has a big investment in you but I agreed out of self-interest to help make the man I love better and my curious thirst to witness such an event. Even if you decide to not become God's prophet, how much fun would it be to be a part of something so amazing? Nobody but you could bring such an eclectic group of characters together. I'm so proud of you."

Luc: "I have always said that love is the greatest inspiration. Gerty, we have some strong competition from Ana. So, what do you say, Barry?"

My first reaction was to tell all three of them no, but when I looked into Ana's eyes, I realized no one could fake that look. Maybe it was nothing more than being blinded by love, but when she smiled, I wanted nothing more than to make her happy and this obviously would make her happy.

Barry: "I want you all to know you are a million miles from convincing me of anything, but I have to admit my curiosity makes this a compelling idea."

I looked over at Ana with a loving smile and said, "Okay, I'll do it."

Gerty: "Great! Luc and I will get everyone together and Ana, you get home and start cooking."

Chapter XVII

The air was filled with delightful smells. Ana was busy in her kitchen mixing and stirring her magic potions for the meal of meals. It never occurred to me to ask her what she was cooking, because I trusted that no matter what it was, it would be a feast fit for kings. I sat in the living room, reading over my memoirs and making notes for the big event. I was still not willing to even consider this foolishness of me being a prophet, but I was looking forward to the dinner and the opportunity to listen to and participate in this summit of minds and ideas.

I was in deep thought when I felt lips touch my neck. I looked around and Ana was smiling.

Barry: "How's the dinner coming? It smells like

a symphony."

Ana: "The conductor needed a break. How are you doing?"

Barry: "Just preparing my eyes, ears, and voice for the meeting of the minds and feeling a bit overwhelmed and nervous."

Ana: "We have time before everyone comes. Let me help you deal with the stress."

She came around the sofa, straddled my legs, and sat on my lap. She smiled and began to unbutton my shirt, kissing my chest after every button she freed from its shackle. Between buttons, she spoke.

Ana: "After all that has happened, this may not be the best time to say this, but everyone has already told you and I want to confirm it. I love you, Barry. I've always loved you. I understand that it may sound like this is part of God's plot, but you have to trust me when I say, it's always been you. Didn't you ever wonder why I never married and had a family? It's because, way back then, you set the bar so high, no man, or woman, ever came close to making me feel how I felt with you."

I believed her. I didn't believe anyone else here in Heaven, but I believed her. We kissed and began a slow process of removing each other's clothes. In the history of man, no greater feeling had ever been felt by humans than the combination of love and passion. Neither one of them could ever equal the feeling one got from both.

Just as our passion reached a new height, Heaven let me down again with a knock at the front door. Ana jumped off my lap, began buttoning up her top, and said, "You better get that. It might be one of the guests. I'm going to run into the bathroom and straighten myself up."

I was leisurely straightening myself up when they knocked a second time. I figured I had better hurry, but in my haste, I buttoned the top button of my shirt in the wrong hole. With no time to fix it, I opened the door. There stood Jesus with a beautiful woman on his arm.

Barry: "Jesus Christ, you're early. I mean, please come in and have a seat."

Jesus: "I hope you don't mind, I brought Mary with me. You did mention inviting her when we talked, and after all, she was my favorite Apostle and the love of my life. I'm sure she will bring a unique perspective to the conversation."

Barry: "Hello, Mary, I'm Barry. Ana will be out in a minute. I just want to say, you are always welcome here. Both of you."

Mary: "Thank you, Barry. Not just for your kind words, but for everything you have done for Jesus. He's a new man and the one I always knew he could be. For that, I will always be in your debt."

Looking down at my wardrobe malfunction, she continued, "Did we interrupt you? We could go for a walk and come back in a little while. For the first time, we enjoy walking around Heaven."

Barry: "Not at all. Please, come in."

Mary hesitated for a moment until Jesus gave her a slight tug forward on her arm. The three of us walked into the living room just as Ana came out.

Barry: "Sweetheart, you remember Jesus, this is Mary Magdalene. Mary, this is the love of my life, Ana."

Ana: "Hello, Jesus, it's nice to see you again. We've been so busy getting ready for this evening, Barry hasn't had time to tell me about his conversation with you. I'm always excited to hear about his adventures. Mary, it is my greatest pleasure to meet you. You are, to me, the original standard-bearer for independent women."

Mary: "Thank you, Ana, but I'm just a woman (like you), who loves her man (like you) and wants him to be everything he can be (like you). I have no interest in being someone special to the world, I just want to be special to him and honest to myself. I'm content being that person behind the curtain."

Ana: "Oh, but you're so much more than just a person behind the curtain. You're the first and only female Apostle. That's huge! You are an inspiration to all women and it's an honor to meet you, but I had better get back to the kitchen before my meal turns to coal."

Jesus: "Oh please, can I join you in the kitchen? It's been millennia since I have smelled such delightful aromas, and I've always wanted to learn to cook, but never had the time. Would I be bothering you if I came in and watched? I could even help if you need water to be boiled. That's about all I'm good at."

Ana: "I would love for you to join me. I have some wonderful wine we can share while we're cooking, and I could use a sous-chef."

Jesus looked giddy as he followed Ana into the kitchen, stopping for a second to turn back at Mary, smiling like a child who has been allowed to play with a broom.

Mary: "He's a different man since he got his haircut from you. He's fun, laughs all the time. It seems like thousands of pounds have been lifted off his shoulders."

Barry: "Haircuts can do that."

Mary: "It was more than just the haircut. Don't get me wrong, I love the haircut, but it's something else. I can't put my finger on it, but it's something you said. He has always been this person at home when we are alone, but outside, he was a frightened little child. He never wanted to go out and we had no friends. Now, he can't get enough of people. He walks through Heaven with a smile on his face. He's a completely different person, and you are responsible for it."

Barry: "I can't imagine anything I did to change him. I guess the haircut gave him newfound freedom he has never had before. Over the years, I have seen, many times, how something as insignificant as a haircut has turned people from a rock into a precious stone. I used to volunteer at the VA hospital once a month cutting the hair of the patients and the homeless. I saw the smiles when they saw themselves in the mirror. It gave them a whole new confidence. You could see in their eyes a glow they didn't have when they came in. It was the greatest joy of my life, so I can understand how powerful something as simple as a haircut can be. By the way, has God seen his haircut yet?"

Mary: "He loved it. He was beaming with pride. Not only because he picked you to cut it, but that His son stood up and did what he wanted."

As Mary and I talked, we could hear Jesus and Ana in the kitchen, giggling like school children.

Mary: "Sounds like Jesus has made his first friend."

Barry: "I can't believe that he hasn't any friends."

Mary: "Not any real friends. Oh, there are lots of people who like him because he's God's son, but none of them treat him like just one of the guys. Can you imagine how it must feel to be loved for what you are, not who you are? It breaks my heart! That's all changed since he got his haircut from you. I recognize it and so does God."

Barry: "I'm glad I could help, but all I did was what any halfway good barber would do. I'm not anything special, just a barber."

Mary: "Jesus was just a carpenter."

Barry: "Yeah, and look what mankind did to him, and I'm not the Son of God. If anyone tried to take Jesus's place, who would help them? God? He didn't do much to help his own son. What could you expect Him to do for someone that isn't His son?"

Mary: "Well, I can't argue with that. He didn't give Jesus much of a chance to spread the word. Of course, if He hadn't sent him to Earth, we might have never met. Sometimes, I think that His real intention was for me to meet Jesus. You know, God doesn't think or plan like us. While we think about our day-to-day tasks, He thinks in one big picture."

Barry: "But what about His precious free will? It sounds to me like He is manipulating us like a little girl does her dolls."

Mary: "It's not that He's manipulating us. At least, I don't think so. It's that everything we are doing is part of an original plan. What happens now or tomorrow was predetermined, just like those video games I see the kids on Earth play. There are points in our lives where we can turn right or left, each leading to a different set of outcomes. That's all the free will we have. What He doesn't want us to do is intervene in His plan, because that would show that He didn't get it right in the first place. That He's imperfect. But now and then, man creates and wanders off, onto his own path. I doubt wars, starvation, or slavery were part of His Grand Plan, but He still refuses to intervene in these mongrel sojourns. I think, just maybe, that's because all roads lead to the same destination."

Barry: "So, you're saying that God's ego is so big that He can't admit to making a mistake. That's not a very good example for His children."

Mary: "It's not about His ego. The fact of the matter is the existence of Heaven, Earth, and the universe is based on the worldly notion that God is infallible and His plan is perfect. If doubt was to ever penetrate this perfect illusion, all this would cease to exist. God himself would cease to exist. He has to do whatever is necessary to maintain, at least, a perception of infallibility."

Barry: "This whole thing sounds messed up. How in the world can this be sustained with all those variables? Seems like the whole thing is impossible and God has bitten off more than He can chew."

Mary: "I agree. Being with Jesus for all this time, I speak to God a lot and I can say there are times when He sounds like He'd just as soon throw it all in a grave and be done with it, but He keeps on doing it. I asked Him once, why He keeps trying. He said because failure isn't an option."

Barry: "Can I ask you a favor?"

Mary: "What would that be?"

Barry: "Will you participate in the discussion today? I think you have an interesting perspective. I want to hear other opinions on what you just told me. That is if you don't mind getting in the dirt with these guys."

Mary: "I guess I'm nothing more than what they call a tomboy. I have no problem and thrive on staring down contrarian opinions. Keep in mind though, none of us know what God's intentions are. The best any of us can do is guess."

Just then, Jesus entered the room with a big smile on his face and a glass of wine in one hand and a pitcher of water in the other. He appeared to be a bit tipsy.

Jesus: "Barry, I want to thank you for inviting us over. I'm having the best time. Ana is so talented, and if her meal tastes as good as it smells, you are the luckiest man I know. Not that I know that many men."

He laughed as though he had said something funny, but the fact of the matter was, I didn't think he knew many men. Still, hearing him laugh felt good, and if I had something to do with that, as Mary suggested, then I felt very proud to have helped him. Just then, Ana came out of the kitchen holding her wine in one hand and two empty wine glasses in the other.

Ana: "It seemed unfair of Jesus and I, enjoying ourselves and excluding you two. Jesus, show Barry that trick you showed me."

She handed the empty glasses to Mary and me with a look of Wait until you see this on her face.

Ana: "Would you do the honors, Jesus?"

Jesus: "I know Mary likes white wine, what would you prefer, Barry?"

Barry: "If you don't mind, I prefer red."

Jesus took the pitcher of water and poured it into Mary's glass. The water turned into white wine in Mary's glass and red in mine.

Ana: "Cool trick, isn't it Barry?"

Jesus looked so proud of what he had just done.

Jesus: "I learned that from my Dad."

With that, Ana raised her glass for a toast.

Ana: "Here's to good food, good libations, and good friends."

As we tapped our glasses together, some spilled out of my glass and onto a rug.

Barry: "I am so sorry, Ana. Let me clean that up. I know a couple of tricks that should work."

Jesus: "No, allow me."

He sat his glass on the table, looked down at the spot, snapped his fingers, and it disappeared.

Barry: "You're just full of tricks. Can you pull a rabbit out of your hat too?"

Mary: "Well, he is the Son of God. He does have powers, although he has never used them in front of anyone in Heaven before. They do come in quite handy around our house. I haven't had to clean the house in a millennium."

Ana, in an attempt to hide her astonishment, suggested that Jesus teach me that trick.

Jesus: "It's pretty easy. All Barry has to do is become the Son of God."

Barry: "No disrespect, but I think I'll stick to my rag and soda water."

The wine continued to flow, and laughter filled the room until Ana excused herself to go back to the kitchen, explaining there was still much to prepare and the dangers of her neglect of the task at hand.

Jesus: "I would offer to help you, Ana, but both of us know I'm nothing more than a distraction. Besides, I'm concerned that if I leave Mary alone with Barry for much longer, he might try to steal her heart. I'm sure she has already stolen his."

Ana: "Well, I don't think so. At least I hope not."

Ana left to go back to the kitchen as the laughter reached a deafening level. I hated to step on such a joyous moment, but I was there to get answers.

Barry: "I want to ask you something, Jesus. If you had a do-over, would you change anything in your time on Earth?"

Jesus: "Yeah, I would have stayed a carpenter. A noble profession where you can see the fruits of your labor. I feel like I accomplished nothing as the Son of God. At least nothing that lasted. Look at the world today. My Father has given them so much and they still aren't satisfied or happy. I guess enough is never enough for man."

Barry: "You don't sound very hopeful for us to figure it all out."

Jesus: "I have to admit, I'm not, and sometimes I think my Father feels the same way."

Mary: "Jesus, you shouldn't say such things, especially since you don't know that for a fact."

Barry: "If He has given up, why put together this elaborate scheme for my benefit?"

Jesus: "Good question, but you always seem to have good questions. I don't know the answer and I doubt anyone else, but my Father, does either. You will have to ask Him when you meet Him."

Barry: "Okay, but when will that be? How much

longer do I have to wait?"

Jesus: "He will come soon."

I was about to ask him how he knew that when the front doorbell rang. I went to the door and there was Mark Twain and Gerty. I invited them in and noticed Peter, Freud, and Lucifer coming up the walk. One by one, everyone arrived. I invited all of them in and Jesus offered them their choice of wine (using his pitcher of water). Lucifer kiddingly asked if I was trying to loosen their tongues with the wine. I was about to deny it but decided to just smile. As all the greetings were exchanged, Ana came in and announced that dinner would be ready in just a few minutes.

Looking around the room, I saw a mélange of great minds, like my days on Earth. I was confident that one of these people (or angel) would surely have the answer to all of my questions. Now, it was up to me, as Stephen said, to ask the right questions, and my mind was racing with questions. But first dinner.

With impeccable timing and a flair for etiquette, Ana entered the room and announced bon appetit. As everyone found their seat, Ana set down plates of different hors-d'oeuvres. I asked if we should say grace and Mark Twain blurted out, "Is Grace here?" as he helped himself to the puttanesca. Gerty quickly elbowed him as she reached for the polenta. Lucifer explained that angels don't eat but commented how really good it all smelled. I looked over at Carlo and saw a tear running down his cheek. I asked if he was all right, and he smiled and said that the food reminded him of the village he came from. Peter and Freud quietly helped themselves, while John just stared at the food, asking what it was he was putting down his gullet. Ana explained that it was baked goat cheese puttanesca with crostini and polenta bites with basil pesto. Will Rogers was cautious with his first bite, explaining that he was more of a steak-and-potatoes guy, but after his first taste, he quickly got into the spirit of the meal. Jesus and Mary served themselves tiny portions while Stephen Hawking filled his plate.

Throughout the history of man, it has been said that the quality of a meal is equal to the volume of the conversation at the table. Silence being the best example of approval and at that moment, if not for the sound of the crostini being chewed, you could hear a pin drop. Just as everyone was finishing up the last few appetizers, Ana returned with a tureen of soup and began to distribute it amongst the guests. Her cream of zucchini seemed to be as Heavenly as her hors-d'oeuvres. Lucifer gave a long breathy sigh of frustration over the aroma, while the others put their heads down to tackle the work at hand. An abundance of moans of approval filled the room, but not a single word.

Ana looked over at me and motioned for me to help her in the kitchen. After a short tutorial on how to balance dishes on my forearms, we returned with the main course. At first glance, Will asked where the meat was.

Ana: "I was thinking of Genesis 1:30 – 'I have given every green plant for food.' So, I decided to make a beef bourguignon, but with mushrooms rather than meat. Does it taste okay, Mr. Rogers?"

Will: "Well, I am reminded of the story about the mountain lion. After eating an entire bull, a mountain lion felt so good he started roaring. He kept it up until a hunter came along and shot him dead... The moral: when you're full of bull, keep your mouth shut."

The room filled with laughter for a short moment and then went silent again with mouths full. Ana's meal was a huge success. When it came time for dessert, it was agreed by all to wait, and that a café carajillo would be a perfect finish.

So, the stage was set, and Ana leaned over, kissed me on the cheek, and whispered in my ear, "They're all yours."

Chapter XVIII

Barry: "So, who wants to answer this? Why has God put all this energy into me?"

The abruptness of my question caught everyone by surprise. I admit it might have been a little more polite to let everyone's food settle, but I have always felt that if you catch people off guard, they won't have time to come up with a convenient answer but instead of getting an answer, everyone just sat there, waiting for someone else to start the discussion. I decided to direct the question to someone specific, and Peter seemed to be the most obvious.

Barry: "Peter, you work closer to God than anyone else here. What's His plan?"

Peter: "Barry, that's like asking a secretary what

his boss's business plan is. I'm confident He has a plan, but I have no idea what it is. A boss never confides secrets to his secretary. I like you and I wish I could be more help, but I can't pretend to know what is going on in the Lord's mind."

Barry: "Does anyone want to chime in on this topic? How about you, Luc, you have faced both God's love and wrath. You exercised your free will and paid highly for it. Does God really believe in man (and angels) having such an empowering gift, or is it all a ruse to give us an illusion of individualism?"

Luc: "Good question, and one I wouldn't hesitate to answer if I knew the answer. You will be wasting your time if you have any expectations that I know what God is thinking or what His Grand Plan is. That was created before any of us were even here. On occasion, I know He tweaks his plan a little and when He does, He asks me to help in a very small way, but I'm nothing more than a subcontractor who works on a small part, but doesn't know what it's being used for."

Barry: "Well, can't you take what you know and make an educated guess?"

Luc: "I learned the hard way that educated guesses can get you in a world of trouble. Now that I'm back in Heaven, I just do what God asks me to do and be happy that I was asked."

Gerty: "And they call women the weaker sex? Ha! I would never be so afraid of anyone or anything that I would blindly participate in whims. Not even God's. I am loyal only to myself and my beloved Alice."

Luc: "I wouldn't expect anything more from you, Gerty. We all know Gerty is about Gerty. That's the only place that there's any there, there in your mind. And if you want a war of words, I'm more than willing to oblige you. You certainly don't scare me, just God."

Gerty: "Oh shut up, Lucifer! God's not here. You can be yourself and this is not being yourself. You may not be whom the Bible says you are, but you sure enjoy playing that role. You have to know His plan. You're His favorite angel. I mean, you mocked Him and His plan and what did He do? He let you back into Heaven."

Luc: "I don't care what you think. He made me and He can end me, and I like being here. I don't know His plans, and ignorance is bliss. If you know something the rest of us don't, Gerty, say it or shut up."

Barry: "I'm sorry, but both of you shut up. This isn't about the two of you, it's about me and God's plan for me. Does anyone have anything to offer besides childish bickering?"

Ana leaned over and whispered in my ear that maybe this wasn't such a good idea. I just smiled, grabbed her hand, and winked to comfort her concerns.

Carlo: "I'm sorry you wasted such a wonderful meal on me, but the truth of the matter is that my contribution to God and Heaven is to trick people. I don't pay attention to the reasons; I just do my job. I love to bullshit people and watch them soak it up. That's all I'm good for. That's all I've ever been good for."

He paused for a moment to look down at his plate, then looked up and continued, "Ana, my mother was the greatest cook that ever lived, but if she had never touched a pentole, that honor would belong to you. Thank you for the best meal I've eaten since I was a child. Barry, I realize I must be a great disappointment to you, but you had to know all along that I was nothing more than a worker ant. A powerful one, who can carry a thousand times his weight, but nevertheless, a worker ant. God likes me. He thinks what I do is funny, but I'm nothing more to Him than a court jester, and you never make the jester the il consultatore."

Even though Carlo Ponzi's whole life had been spent tricking people, I began to think he actually might be the most honest of the lot. There was something innocent about him. He did what he did because it was what he did best. If only more people were as satisfied in their skin as he was in his. I thanked Carlo for his honesty and turned to John Lennon, knowing I would probably hit another wall.

Barry: "John, can you add anything to this very uninformative conversation?"

John: "Being a misanthrope since coming here and having only recently wandered out onto the streets of Heaven, I'm reminded that the more I see, the less I know. But what I do know is you are far more than just a barber. You have a voice that resonates with people. Being one who had a resonating voice on Earth, I can say it is a dangerous attribute. It usually gets you into more trouble than it helps. If you were to decide to pursue this path that God has laid out for you, remember one thing: people don't listen to what you say. They rearrange your words and read between the lines to suit their agenda. That's how I wound up here. I said, 'The Beatles were more popular than Jesus,' but that was intended to be a slap in the face of the fans, not Jesus. Nevertheless, some people saw an opportunity to use it for their own gains by twisting the meaning of my words. Fourteen years after I said those words, I was murdered for them by Chapman. Although I think it's safe to say he did me a favor."

Barry: "What do you mean, he did you a favor?"

John: "After all, everybody loves you when you're six feet in the ground. If you don't believe me, ask anyone here. All of us were worshipped (and still are) by millions of people. Of course, Jesus is worshipped by many more than the rest of us, but our words have become Scripture to mankind. I can't tell you what God's plan is, but I can tell you that you should fear religion, not God. Religion survives on the laziness of man to have all his questions about life asked for him by someone else and accepts their answers as The Word. I doubt this helps you make sense of what you are going through, but if you follow through with what appears to be God's plan, remember, it is the insurmountable truth."

Barry: "Actually, John, it helps a lot. If you looked in the box labeled Cowards, you'd see me waving up at you. I have no interest in being a martyr. Either by accident or on purpose."

I looked over at Freud and asked, "Am I wrong, Dr. Freud? Am I missing something?"

Sigmund: "No one can tell you what to do, but what I will say is if indeed, God has a plan for you, no matter what it is, you can only do one of two things. Either prepare for the inevitable or prepare for a journey into the unknown."

Barry: "What do you mean, and how do I do that?"

Before he could answer, the doorbell rang. Ana

went to answer the door, while we all waited to see who it might be. I thought, could it be God? The answer came quickly.

Ana: "I was thinking you can never have too many opinions, so I invited someone I met recently that I thought just might bring some light to this conversation."

There, standing next to her was a short black man with a tranquil smile and compassionate eyes.

Ana: "For those who don't know him, I would like you to meet my new friend, Dr. Martin Luther King, Jr."

Dr. King: "It is my greatest honor to be invited to a group of such distinguished minds. Ana, I'm sorry I missed dinner. From what I've been told, your dinners are not just meals, but culinary events."

Then, he looked over at me.

Dr. King: "You must be Barry. God's favorite barber and the love of Ana's life. I'm honored to finally meet you. Word has it that you are perplexed by the thought of being God's prophet. Ana thought you might appreciate some input from someone who has been there."

Barry: "You mean you were a prophet of God?"

Dr. King: "Absolutely! Do you remember the story about that woman stabbing me because she thought I was conspiring against her with Communists?

Barry: "Vaguely…"

Dr. King: "Reports were that I almost died from the wound? Well, I did die from it and came here. After being mentored by God Himself, here in Heaven, He sent me back to Earth to be His prophet."

Barry: "I can understand why He would want you to be a prophet. Your MLK Jr. I'm just a barber."

Dr. King: "I was a twenty-six-year-old pastor of a small red church in Alabama when I died the first time. I was simply a young man following God's Word, or what I thought was God's Word. He had become extremely anxious and angry at what His experiment had become and wanted things to change. He made me who I became, and He will do the same for you if, indeed, that is His plan."

Barry: "I think it's just nuts for Him to think I have any special talent that can bring man together. That is so above my pay grade."

Dr. King: "That's exactly how I felt when I found out about His plan for me."

Barry: "And you just accepted it? I won't do that. I love being right where I am, with Ana, and have zero interest in going back to Earth."

Dr. King: "Well, that's between you and God, but don't expect to win that argument. I speak from experience. He will surely try to convince you to go willingly, but if that doesn't work, He will command it."

Barry: "What about my free will?"

Dr. King: "At this point, He is ready to throw free will to the wind. Man has abused it, and His patience has run out."

He paused in thought.

Dr. King: "You're a very lucky guy, Barry. This is the perfect time to be His prophet. There will be no games and only one message to man. Either straighten up and fly right or face the consequences."

Barry: "And what will those consequences be, exactly?"

Dr. King: "That's a good question, and I wish I knew the answer. What I do know is that man has pushed God to the brink and that can't be a good thing."

Barry: "So what do you think He will do, and how am I a part of it?"

Dr. King: "He's capable of anything, but what He will do is a different story. If you truly are God's prophet, you are a very lucky one. This time, there will be no subtleties like in the past. He has given them the seven warnings and they ignored every single one of them. He sent His Son and then me and they turned their backs on both of us. They are more obsessed with their free will, and it has become so important to them that they have forsaken God's message. Religion has been highjacked by charlatans who have put their words above God's Word, interpreting His word of love into fear, hate, greed, and selfishness. They have fooled most good men (and women) to follow a path that will never lead them to this promised land. These charlatans are the true serpents and He's had enough. His Bible is just one Word, and that Word is love. Until I came here, I believed that the Bible was His Word, but it was nothing more than a series of parables written to scare and control man by other men. Mr. Lennon is right. Man is fundamentally lazy. Most are followers, and although they claim their free will is important, they're much more comfortable as common lemmings."

Being suspicious of almost everyone, I jumped in.

Barry: "How did you know what John said? You weren't here when he said it."

Dr. King: "I'm so very sorry. Since I was late, I sat at the door for a few minutes and listened to the conversation, so I could be helpful when I came in."

He sounded sincere, so I simply smiled and shook my head in approval. Just as he was about to continue his thoughts, some of the others wanted to add their two cents' worth into the conversation.

Carlo: "This gift God has given us was intended to make us all better people. Better as a parent, better as brothers or sisters, better as friends, and better as a neighbor, and we distorted it to make it all about ourselves. What a waste of a perfectly good gift."

Will: "It seems to me that freedom never works as well in practice as it does in conversation. We preach and fight for our personal liberty, but we never think, nor do we care, about how that individual freedom affects the freedom of others."

Freud: "But most people don't want that freedom because it involves responsibility, and most people are afraid that if left to their own devices, they might make the wrong decision. It's safer to let others make those choices for them."

Stephen: "Free will? Oh, please! What an illusion. The only free will man has is to hate, fear, or love. Everything man does comes down to one of those three choices and only one of them is God's way. So, where's the free will?"

Barry: "I appreciate all these comments, but that's not why I asked you all here. I want to know what you think about me being God's prophet."

Twain: "I feel the need to throw a stone rather than coal into the brazier. What makes you think God wants you to be His prophet? Have you met Him since we last spoke?"

Barry: "Well, no, but according to Lucifer, that's what all this has been about."

Luc: "Maybe I'm wrong. I've been wrong before. Remember, I'm the one that thought He would laugh at my joke. It seemed like the logical answer, but we all know that God doesn't think like we do."

Barry: "So, you don't really know, do you? It was just more of your tricks and lies."

Luc: "Barry, I just told you I didn't know. I'm a muse. If there is anything that stands in the way of a muse doing his job, it's tricks and lies. My job is to bring the best out of someone, and I can't do that without their trust."

Dr. King: "Don't be too hard on Luc, Barry. I can honestly say that no one here is tricking or lying to you and none of us know what God's plan is for you. I'm sure whatever it is, God has given it a lot of consideration and it's been in His plan for millenniums. If indeed, you are His choice of a prophet, I can honestly say it will be different this time. He has grown so disgusted with man, He will surely take a more hands-on approach. This time it won't be allegories and idle threats. This time, the threats will be real. Personally, I would love to be in your shoes."

I felt I had let Ana down. I looked over at her and with a combination of sadness and frustration in my voice.

Barry: "What a waste of your precious time, Ana. You worked so hard to make everything perfect. I'm sorry it didn't turn out like we hoped it would."

Ana: "I'm not sorry at all. Just because we

don't know what God's plan for you might be, I think it's safe to say we know there is a plan. I'm sure it's only a matter of time, and He will answer all your questions."

Dr. King: "And I can also safely add that you'll know very soon what His plan is."

Barry: "How can you say that with so much confidence?"

Dr. King: "Because He's waiting for you at your barbershop."

Chapter XIX

Barry: "Should I go now?"

Peter: "Probably not a good thing to keep Him waiting too long. He's not known for His patience."

Barry: "Well, what do I say? I mean…can I ask Him questions? I have so many questions to ask."

Dr. King: "He's expecting you to ask questions and will answer them honestly whether you like the answers or not. I guess when you're as powerful as God, you don't really care if people don't like the answers. Anyway, you had better get going."

Ana: "You want me to go with you? I would love to meet God."

Dr. King: "I'm sorry, Ana, but God wants to talk

to Barry alone right now. Those were His orders."

I assured her I'd be okay, but as I walked down the walkway, I felt like my heart would burst through my chest. I began to think, I have to organize my thoughts before I reach the shop. After all, God must be very busy and doesn't have the patience for a potpourri of jumbled questions. Also, I should be respectful and not confrontational. But then I thought, God, knows me. He knows everything. He will see right through that. I have spent my entire life challenging people to prove to me they're right. I should challenge Him? I mean, what can He do to me if I stand up to Him and use the free will he so generously gave me?

Then I remembered what he could do, and what he did do to Luc. I didn't want to wind up being cast away from Heaven, like Luc, for even a single day. Right now, I couldn't imagine a day going by that Ana wasn't at my side. I didn't know what to do, so I did what I always did when confronted with a dilemma. I found a very flat stone on the ground, decided which side was heads, and flipped it into the air. Heads respectful, tails confrontational. It bounced a few times on the ground and finally settled with tails up.

The die was cast and all that was left was to find out exactly what God's plan was and what I had to do with it. I wondered, would this first meeting be a negotiation or a command on what lay ahead? If indeed I was to be His next messenger, His prophet, would it be more of the same or did He plan a different approach this time? As I approached the barbershop, I became acutely aware, for the first time what real fear felt like.

I entered the shop and there sitting in one of the big, comfy, vintage mid-century barber chairs, was a small man with a big friendly smile, longish and unruly hair, a long beard that screamed of neglect, wearing rimless glasses. It seemed obvious this wasn't God.

Barry: "Hello, sir, I'm sorry if you have been waiting long for a haircut, but I'm expecting God at any moment, so I'll have to ask you to come back later."

His smile got a little bit bigger as he said, "What were you expecting Me to look like, Barry?"

Barry: "You're God?"

God: "I guess you could say I'm God's avatar, but yes, it's Me. I don't have a body, so this is the best I can do."

Barry: "Forgive me for not knowing it was you, but quite honestly, this avatar is not what I was expecting."

God: "My bad, I thought this might be a bit less intimidating. What were you expecting?"

Barry: "I don't know, but certainly not this."

In the blink of an eye, the little man turned into a handsome swashbuckling Errol Flynn-looking character.

God: "Is this better? Like one of your Walter Mitty dreams, huh?"

I couldn't help but laugh. Luc was right; He did have a sense of humor.

Barry: "I guess that works, although it doesn't really matter. What does matter is what do I call You? I have a thousand questions, and I want to be respectful and call You by Your name."

God: "Now that's a problem. You see, I don't have a name. No reason for one, since I'm God, the only God, but if you want to call Me something, call me Sam."

Barry: "Sam? Why Sam? I mean, is there any significance to calling You, Sam?"

God: "There seems to be a dispute amongst humans as to whether I'm a man or a woman. Since I'm both, the Heavenly Father and Mother Nature, Sam seems to be a good name. Depending on the moment and the issue, I can be either Samuel or Samantha."

Barry: "Well, Sam, with all due respect, let's go straight to the punch line. What is Your plan and what is my role in it? I've been told by Luc that Your plan includes me as Your prophet."

God: "Well, Barry, it's true that My plan includes you, but not as a prophet. Don't take this wrong, but you're not prophet material."

Barry: "That's what I've been telling everyone. I'm just a barber and will always be just a barber. I'm happy being a barber."

God: "As well, you should. There's absolutely nothing wrong with being a barber. It's an honorable profession. Joseph was just a carpenter and look at his contribution to the world. In fact, you being a barber is very important to My plan. I don't want you to be anything more than that."

Barry: "So, what is Your plan for me, do I have any say in it or is it an order from on high?"

God: "Of course, you have a say in it, but let Me ask you something first. Would you say you learned anything since you've been a barber here in Heaven? I mean, did all those people I sent to get their haircut make an impact on you? Do you think you're, shall we say, more enlightened by their appearance here in your shop?

Barry: "Absolutely!"

God: "On a scale of one to ten, what would you give it?"

Barry: "I guess somewhere around eight or nine out of ten. I mean, most of them were very enlightening, but then there was Freud. I didn't agree with almost everything he said. He seemed rather full of himself."

God: "I agree that I may have dropped the ball on Freud. So, who was your favorite?"

Barry: "Well, at first I thought either Mark Twain or Will Rogers was, but recently I've been thinking Carlo Ponzi. He seems the most honest, in a most dishonest way."

God laughed a great belly laugh and said, "He's My favorite too. He makes no excuses for who he is, and in a way, that makes him very honorable."

Barry: "Yeah, except like all the others, he had no answers to my questions. I asked all of them and no one could help me get clarity. All I've gotten from them were riddles and question marks. Made me feel like I was just a toy in Your toy box."

God: "You're not a toy at all. You're very important to Me. I think it's time I be straight with you."

Barry: "I would appreciate a little honesty right about now. What is Your plan and how do I fit in?"

God: "By the way, I read your manuscript, and you've become a pretty good writer. You're no Mark Twain, but then there's only one Mark Twain, but I agree with what Gertrude said; there is definitely some there, there. Anyway, you want an explanation? Okay, here we go. Have a seat, this won't take long."

Finally, some answers to my questions. I sat down in the other barber chair, leaned back, and looked right into the eyes of His buccaneer avatar.

God: "My grand plan has become a monstrous failure. I thought I could create this world and sit back, and it would run itself. And it did for a short time, but after a while, humans stopped asking questions, and after all, there are no answers without questions. That's why I picked you. You understand the importance of the question. Man, for the most part, has become very lazy and relied on a handful of other men to provide them with a message, but their message is not My message. The majority of humans are no longer members of My flock. Instead, they have come to revere these unworthy charlatans that have poisoned the real message with their fear, hate, jealousy, envy, and greed for personal gains. My message is simple. All I asked from man was to love each other, but all these 'man-made' traits have woven themselves into the narrative. These negative traits have created a monstrosity (as Luc once called it) and the time has come for Me to intervene. When I sent Jesus down to Earth the first time, I thought his presence would be enough. He promised to return, but I never really thought it would be necessary. My plan was for Heaven and Earth to be one, but I missed that target. This time, I'm going to be hands-on, and if mankind doesn't straighten its act out, it could get ugly."

Barry: "What do you mean by ugly?"

God: "Excuse My French, but I'm pissed off. Really pissed off! I've grown tired of man's self-centeredness. They have turned My gift of free will into an abomination. They only want to use it for their personal gains and expect Me to fix all the problems they create. They just don't get it. Free will means free from Me, and science is the solution for that. I gave man the ability to ask questions that would help find the answers on his own. My plan has always been for them to be independent. Questions lead to discovery and create true independence. Man would still be living in the cold, with no fire to keep him warm, if it weren't for questions and discovery, yet most have drunk the snake oil the mountebanks have sold them and believe questions and science to be the tools of some sort of evil nemesis. The dumb schmucks haven't figured out that there is no devil or demons except themselves.

I've run out of patience with him. Either man will start flying right, or I will hit the control-alt-delete keys on them and their precious Earth. I don't want to do that, but I won't hesitate another moment if they don't change their ways. After all, Earth is not My only experiment. There are millions of others, and one less will not change much in My grand plan."

Barry: "Respectfully, a lot of what You say is because You haven't been a good father. Like my father was with me, you weren't there through man's formative years. Maybe you were busy, but it seems to me that You only showed up when we made You angry and was never there with encouragement for our good behavior. You left us to make up our own rules and when You didn't like those rules, You threatened instead of guiding us. With the greatest respect, one could make the argument that You have been a deadbeat dad."

God: "You have learned well from your mentors. There have been long stretches where I have been M.I.A. I hoped that man would figure it out for himself, but now I see I was wrong."

Barry: "Once again, respectfully, You expected humans to be perfect, but You're not perfect yourself. You just told me You're angry. Isn't anger a flaw in one's character?"

God: "That's what I like about you, Barry. You don't pull punches. You're right. Man would love for Me to be perfect. He has always thought of his God (or gods) as perfect, but no one gets around the Yin-Yang of life. Not even Me. I also agree that I have been a bit of a deadbeat dad, but I'm here now and I'm ready to be hands-on."

I couldn't believe I was saying these things to God. Was I nuts or was there something He did to me that brought out this honesty? No matter what it was, I might as well continue. He seemed to be appreciating what I was saying.

God: "So, here's my deal, Barry. I'm going to send you back to Earth thirty years ago before you died, and you will lead my new plan."

Barry: "You can do that?"

God: "Einstein got it right when he said time is an illusion. That the dividing line between past, present, and future is nothing more than a figment of the imagination. Besides, I'm God with a capital G. I can do anything I want."

Barry: "So I am going to be Your prophet?"

God: "No, I wouldn't do that to you. Your job is to be the father of my prophet. It's time for Jesus to return like I said he would and now, thanks to you, I think he's ready for the task at hand."

Barry: "No!"

God: "What do you mean, no?"

Barry: "No means no. I won't go back. I want to stay here with Ana. I love her and won't leave her for a single day. You want a fix-it man, find someone else."

God: "When you're right, you're right."

Barry: "What are You saying?"

Just then, the door opened, and Ana walked in.

Ana: "Peter and Martin told me that God wanted to talk to me too, so here I am. What's going on?"

Barry: "God wants me to leave you and go back to Earth and be the father of Jesus."

Ana: "So where is she?"

Barry: "Who"

Ana: "God!"

God raised his hand like a child who had the answer to the teacher's question.

Ana: "With all due respect, I wasn't expecting you to look like a character out of Pirates of the Caribbean."

God: "It's a long story.

He looked back at me.

God: "First, I never said I wanted you to leave Ana. After all, Jesus will need a mother too, won't he?"

A look of complete confusion came over Ana's face.

Ana: "So, let me get this straight. You want Barry and me to go back to Earth and be the parents of Your son?"

God: "Bingo! The first time he was there, he was the son of a carpenter and his wife. This time, he will be the son of a barber...and a chef. You will raise him from the lessons you have learned here and when he has grown up, I will take over and you will return to Heaven and pick up where you left off. No harm, no foul!"

Barry: "And if we say no thanks?"

Ana: "Yeah, Jesus and Mary have become our friends and we won't be a part of anything that will cause him pain like he endured the last time he was there.

God: "Then I guess there will be no future for mankind. As I told Barry, my patience has run out. This time, I won't be playing games or giving hints. I plan on being hands-on until man either straightens up or earth is no more."

Barry: "And how do you plan to do that?"

God: "I will be right there in the barbershop next to you, guiding you and Ana. And, your customers up here, will become your customers down there. All except Steven. He'd still be alive and duplicating him might confuse people. No one, including you and Ana, will suspect who they are. You won't recognize them, but they will be there to serve as mentors just like they did here. Between all of us and what Will calls a few celestial lariat tricks, the two of you and Jesus should have all the help you need to make it work. And, if it doesn't work, I will simply bring everyone, along with those who are virtuous, back here and leave the rest to face their doom."

Barry: "I want to know something before I say yes or no. Is this a command or am I allowed to use my free will?"

God: "I have to admit I have recently had a change of heart about free will. As much as I want my children to use their free will, I've come to understand that children must learn the alphabet before they can read.

Barry: "So if I say no, will I be sent away or even worse?"

God: "I want you to want to say yes, so let me sweeten the pot. I know how much you have enjoyed cutting the hair of your heroes and other famous men, how 'bout I let you make a list of men whose hair you'd like to cut in Heaven. It would give you an endless supply of material to write about. Also, I've decided it's time there was an ocean in heaven and when you return, there will be a sailboat waiting for you where you can write your memoirs and the two of you can watch the sunset over a glass of wine. So, let me ask you...if you agree, whose hair would you like to cut first?"

Barry: "That sounds awfully enticing. If I were to agree, I think I'd like to cut George Carlin's hair, but I figure he's not in Heaven. He was one of your biggest critics when he was alive."

God: "Remember Peter told you that you'd be surprised who was in Heaven? Well, he's there and he will be waiting at the shop when you get back."

Barry: "I'm on board, but you still have to convince Ana. If she doesn't want to go, I won't go."

God looked over at Ana.

God: "I haven't forgotten you, Ana. If you agree, I will create a restaurant right next to Barry's barbershop and anyone in Heaven can come in and eat. From what I heard about your cooking, once the word gets out, they will be lining up outside to get in."

I looked over at Ana and she looked like a little girl who had gotten a puppy for Christmas. She was smiling from ear to ear.

Barry: "What do you say, sweetheart?"

She was trying to hold back the tears, while still smiling from ear to ear.

Ana: "I don't think I could ever be happy again if I felt responsible for the end of our precious Earth and the idea of cooking for all those people in Heaven is awfully appealing. I say yes!"

Since nothing was more important to me than Ana's happiness, the decision was easy.

Barry: "Okay…we have a deal. When should we plan on this happening?"

God: "Since I've already procrastinated for far too long, how about right now? I promise you won't feel like you've missed a moment. You both will go back in time thirty years, and you will return thirty years later. You won't remember any of this and you will only know Me as your best friend and fellow barber, Sam. Together, all of us will raise Jesus to become the person he needs to be to do My work. You'll return to heaven and I will stay there with him the rest of the way. There will be no dying for their sins crap, no crucifixions, and no resurrections. This is man's last chance to right their ship."

Barry: "Sounds good to me. Are you ready, darling?"

Ana: "I'm ready. Let's do it!"

Chapter XX

It wasn't just another day – it was our last day. When we woke up, the air seemed so fresh and filled with anticipation of our new adventure together. Over the last few years, the passion for our crafts, like our scissors and knives, had become dull, and our love for the smell of bay rum and risotto had been replaced by the warm salty scent of the sea. While most people our age were busy winding down, Ana and I were ready to ramp it up. And like our favorite writer, Mark Twain once said, the time had come to throw off the bowlines and catch the trade winds in our sail.

The time had come to hand the barbershop over to our son, Jesus. I still remember when he was born and how much Ana wanted to name him Jesus. When I asked her why she told me that great things happen to people with great names. I learned early on to never question Ana when her mind was set, so Jesus it was. As a father, I couldn't be prouder. He had worked hard to get to this point, and I was so excited to hand the keys to the shop over to him. Through the years, he had been a barber, he had built a strong clientele and combined with all my crazy old customers (or at least those that were still around), there was no doubt in our minds that he would be successful.

Don't get me wrong, it wasn't that I hated being a barber or Ana a chef. Life was safe in our neat little box. We would go to work, make some money, go home, spend our evenings together, go to bed, get up, and do it all over again. It never occurred to us that we could have done something any more gratifying in our life together than watching our son grow to be a man. Our work also afforded us the time to be hands-on parents to our son as he grew up.

My father, like many others of his day, wore his gray flannel suit with pride and was always too busy working to participate in my growing up, and I didn't want to be like that. As far as I was concerned, no one ever got rich from being a barber, but it allowed me to set my schedule so I could be there in the stands, watching Jesus play in his baseball, basketball, and volleyball games, not to mention all the award ceremonies. It also afforded me the time to teach him the lessons of life, the most important lesson being to question everything, and he learned his lessons well.

Barbering made life pretty simple to be a father, but now, it was time to push Jesus out of the nest, vault over the side of our neat little box, and challenge life. And what better way to do that than on our boat with my beloved Ana, a bottle of wine, looking out at the sunset.

Yeah, it was our last day, but it was also our first day, and the first act of this new day was to deep-six all devices with a common denominator of twenty-four. Time and work were now joining damn and hell as four-letter words.

When Ana and I walked into the shop for the last time, Jesus was sitting, talking to my best friend, Sam. Sam had worked with me at the shop since I opened it thirty years ago and was the best man at our wedding. Although he looked like Errol Flynn, he never got married and found great pleasure in living vicariously through us. I guess one could say he was the patriarch of the family and the one we all turned to for that much-needed common-sense advice. It made leaving Jesus a lot easier for Ana and me, knowing he would be there for him.

Jesus: "Well, look what the cat dragged in, Sam. What do you suggest we do with these two vagrant barn swallows?"

Sam: "I dare say, we should show them pity. After all, their journey is long, and their wagon is badly in need of repair."

We all laughed as Jesus came to Ana, kissed her on the cheek, and hugged her so tight I thought her eyes would pop from her head.

Jesus: "I'm gonna miss you guys so much!"

Ana: "We're gonna miss you too, both of you, but especially you, my sweet son."

Jesus: "It's not too late, Mom. You can stay. Besides, there's no guarantee that the P.O.S. car of Dad's will even get you to the boat."

Barry: "You wouldn't be trying to steal the love of my life from me, would you, son? Stop worrying, Jesus, the grand plan is perfect. The house is sold, the money is safely stashed away, and all that is left is to hand you the keys, walk out of that door for the last time, and onto the deck of our floating little piece of Heaven."

Jesus: "Well, if I can't talk you into changing your mind, will you at least take an Uber to the boat? That piece of junk outside is a death trap. It sounds like a lawnmower, doesn't even have a working air conditioner, and it's hot as hell out there."

Barry: "We'll be okay. We'll just open the windows and besides, we're taking the coast route, so we can pass one last time by Mom's restaurant."

Ana: "Don't you worry, sweetheart, we'll be fine. You know we've been planning this since you were born. The time is right and besides, you have Sam. Listen to him and do what he tells you and you'll be fine. He's always been there for you and don't think for a moment we won't be there for you anytime you need us. I know it will be a bit scary at times, but we know you will do what you were born to do… whatever it may be."

Just then, Mary walked into the shop. Mary was Jesus's new bride. They had only gotten married a few months earlier, and we loved her like she was our own daughter. She was smart, beautiful, and knew just how to flip his switches. They adored each other and reminded me of Ana and me when we were that age.

Mary: "I'm so happy for the two of you. By the way, I brought along a few people that wanted to say goodbye and wish you luck."

She went to the door, opened it, and motioned for them to come in. One by one, my favorite clients over the years walked in. There was Peter, Luc, Gerty, Carlo, John, Mark, Will, and Martin. The room became filled with so much wisdom, any concerns Ana and I might have had for Jesus disappeared like a small breath of smoke. The range of their wisdom filled the entire spectrum of knowledge. Peter was a minister at the local Methodist church, Luc an entertainment agent, Gerty a book publisher, Carlo a used car salesman, John a Street musician, Mark an author, Will a standup comedian, and Martin a social worker. Since I started cutting their hair, I knew that any questions I might have would eventually be answered by one of them.

Just when I thought it couldn't get any better than this, Mary opened the door again, and in came my mother. Mary and Ana ran over to her to help her get over the threshold. Sam got up and helped them get her into his chair. After Dad passed away a few months ago, Mom hardly left the house and had gone downhill pretty quickly. She was beginning to show signs of dementia, but that day, she knew exactly where she was. Ana loved her like she was her own mother because we would have never found each other again if it wasn't for Mom. Mom always had a big smile on her face when she saw Ana. There were times I thought she might love her more than me, which was just fine.

Mary had outdone herself. Everyone important to us was there. She went into the back room and came out with a bunch of plastic cups and a couple of bottles of champagne. While she handed each of us a cup, Jesus popped the corks and poured. Once everyone's glass was filled, one by one, they held their glasses high. But before the toasts began, I kiddingly asked the Pastor a question.

Barry: "Hey, Peter, tell me one thing. Will I be able to sail in Heaven? I'm not sure I want to go anytime soon if I can't."

Peter: "No one knows for sure what Heaven is like, or when they will experience its glory, but until that time comes, here's to a long and happy life."

Gerty looked over at her wife Alice's hand and grabbed it, saying, "Go out there and dare to be happy. In all my years with my beloved Alice, the only love story I've witnessed that comes close to ours is the two of you, Barry and Ana. Jesus, Mary, learn from their example and never forget, you look ridiculous if you dance, you look more ridiculous if you don't, so you might as well dance."

Then she handed me a leather-bound book. On the front, it read, If Hair Could Talk.

Gerty: "I want twenty pages from you in a month."

Luc: "I never thought I'd say this, but I agree with Gerty. Have fun, grow, and relish every moment together. A step forward is a step up and it brings you one step closer to the top of the mountain. Barry, Ana, you are so close to the top, you can touch it.

Jesus and Mary, simply follow their path and you'll reach the top too. You all have earned it."

Carlo: "Most of you know I'm a salesman. I have lived my life on the power of my ability to bullshit, but for a moment, let me speak from my heart. Barry and Ana, never forget how lucky the two of you are. Not only do you get to live your dream, but you get to live it together. So many people, most people, are never given that opportunity. Never take your love for granted, always keep showing it, and you'll never get bored with it."

John: "The song says love is all you need and there is so much love in this room right now. It's real love, without the fear that attaches itself to most love like a parasite. Be fearless in your new journey and drink up every last drop, as I plan on doing with this fine wine."

Mark: "I have never written about romance. Probably because I was such a failure at it, but watching the two of you over the years, I have come to a whole new appreciation that it is what makes this sometimes-ugly world go round. You both wear your love like a moniker. Not just between the two of you, but with everything and everyone in your lives. Whether it was raising Jesus, cutting hair, or cooking, you always attacked it with love, passion, and even a bit of lust. I'm sure that sailing will be no different, so

I wish you well. Go catch those trade winds in your sails. Explore, discover, and most of all, dream. By the way, where is that quack, Sigmund?"

Mary: "I got the impression that no one liked him but Peter."

Sam: "Peter doesn't count. He likes everyone. I always felt guilty about putting Freud in Barry's chair. I agree with what Mark said about him. He is a pompous, tent show charlatan whose opinions are not worth the paper he wrote them on."

Barry: "Come on, folks, don't you think it's a bit unfair to criticize him when he isn't here to defend himself?"

I paused for a breath and continued, "Having said that…thank you, Mary!"

Mary: "I just remember being here once and having to listen to his dribble and thought to myself, What a douche. Anyway, does anyone else want to toast Barry and Ana?"

Will: "It's been said that rumor travels faster, but it don't stay put as long as truth, so let me speak of truth. I feel honored to have known the two of you for all these years and I wish you luck in this new adventure. And when the time comes for you to move on, I hope you go as peacefully as my father, who died in his sleep…not screaming like all the passengers in his car."

Martin: "I have never had a haircut from you, Barry, and I have never been fortunate to have tasted one of your famous meals, Ana."

Ana smiled and interrupted, "We'll have to fix that, Martin."

Martin: "Thank you, but neither is necessary for me to know all I need to know about the two of you. I know you are living proof that all labor that uplifts humanity has dignity and importance, and you have undertaken it with painstaking excellence. I knew on Saturdays, when I worked with the homeless, once a month like clockwork, the two of you would be there. Ana helped with the cooking and Barry cut hair and you always brought Jesus along. I once asked why you would bring a child to such a sad place, and Ana told me, so he would see the pain in this world and how the simplest things can ease that pain. You are more than parents; you are navigators, plotting a course for Jesus to follow, and your map was not wasted on him, because now I see him there, once a month, cutting hair, just like his father.

"You have taught him with surgical precision that the quality, not the longevity, of one's life, is what is important and the two of you have lived a life where kindness and compassion are the most important elements of the journey. I will miss your monthly visits. I will miss the smiles on the faces when they see their new haircut or their first bite of Ana's meals, but I have Jesus (and Mary) to remind me, and I know your acts of kindness and compassion will keep their memory strong."

Mary: "It's been said that behind every great man is a woman, but I disagree. After getting to know Barry and Ana, I can honestly say that saying is wrong. The two of you have always stood side by side in everything you do. You have taken me into your hearts, not as a daughter-in-law, but like your own daughter. I have never met anyone that loved another like the two of you love each other. I can only hope, pray, and work so that Jesus and I can experience that same compassion you show each other. I love you both so much and although this is not goodbye, it can't be said enough."

Sam: "As I have said many times, science (like life) is predicated on one's failures. We learn from our mistakes, not our successes. If that is true, and I believe it is, it would be safe to say the two of you have learned nothing over the last thirty years. You have succeeded as parents, as lovers, and I know you will find endless success in your future. Years ago, Barry told me I should never become a father if I wasn't willing to devote my life to my child. I wasn't sure what he meant, but I listened to his advice and over the last twenty-five years, he taught me what it is to be a father. I know I will never be one now, but I promise to follow your blueprint with Jesus. Barry, Ana, don't worry, I've got this. Jesus, you are as close to a son as I will ever know, and I promise you and your parents that I will always be by your side. I know you will do great things in your life. Maybe even greater than you or your parents could ever imagine."

Jesus: "You guys are a hard act to follow, but I'll try. Mom, Dad, you have given me such confidence in my life, I feel there is nothing I can't do. I promise I will never rest on my laurels and I will savor every moment of my life. I know it's not that you won't be around, but it is time for me, as Sam would say, to step up to the plate and swing for the wall. To the rest of you, I know I will never be able to fill my dad's shoes, but with your help and support, I think we can leave an impact on this world, even if in a small way. Dad, you taught me to question everything, and Mom, you taught me to love everything. I ask all of you, is there any more to life than that? So, let's raise our glasses to thank both of them for everything they have given us, and I can't wait to hear all about your new adventure."

With that, everyone raised their glasses and said, "To Ana and Barry!" and took a sip. That is, except for Sam. He drank the whole damn glass.

Ana, with tears in her eyes, said, "You know how much all this means to me, but I can't even imagine what it all means to Barry. When I ran into Barry's mom years ago and she invited me for dinner, I almost didn't go. I was worried that he was still mad or hurt at how I had left years earlier, but when he walked me home, he reached for my hand. The rest is history. Mary, don't ever settle for anything but the best from Jesus. Jesus, you already have the best in Mary. Always appreciate her love and work harder every day to earn it.

"Barry, I love you so much! You have always been the guiding light in my tower. Looking back, I don't know what I would have done or where I'd be today if you hadn't reached for my hand that night. You will never know how much I wanted you to. There's a song by Crystal Gayle that if I didn't know better, I'd say was written for us. It goes like this:

Take me home, you silly boy, Put your arms around me.

Take me home you silly boy, All the world's not round without you.

I'm so sorry that I broke your heart, please don't leave my side.

Take me home, you silly boy, 'cause I'm still in love with you.

We did it, sweetheart. Now let's go and raise

that sail and maybe, just a little bit of hell. But as always, together."

Barry: "I'm speechless, but that has never stopped me before. Confucius said, "If you are the smartest person in the room, then you are in the wrong room." Well, I have definitely been in the right room for the last thirty years. I've been blessed to have you people in my life that have served as beacons guiding me through this journey. I would not be where I am if not for every one of you, but without a doubt, it was Ana that has had the biggest impact. To all my friends here, I want to thank you for your kind words and all the advice you've given me through the years. It can be a scary world out there and your wisdom has helped bring calm to the tempestuous seas of my life.

"Sam, I did say you'd be a lousy father, but I was wrong. I couldn't think of anyone who is more qualified to be a father, and we have no hesitation in leaving our son in your hands. Most of you know Sam as my boisterous partner in crime. Some of you might even be a bit scared of him. To you, I want to say, no man I know is more giving, loving, and caring. I will miss our daily chats between haircuts and your endless guidance and advice. At the risk of sounding like a bad Paul Rudd movie, I love you, man.

"Mary, when Jesus met you, it was the luckiest

moment of his life. You are so very special, and I know, with your help and guidance, there is no ceiling to his potential. I know you will stand next to him throughout this journey. There will be times when he will want to throw his hands into the air out of frustration. Those times will be the times he will need you the most. With complete certainty, I know you will be there with the right words and the love to help him to get through it.

"Ana, my love. A famous actor was once asked how much of his success was luck and how much was talent. He replied it was ninety-percent luck, but when luck comes your way, you have to be ready. You came to me once, and I wasn't ready. The next time, I made sure I was. Reaching for your hand was the hardest thing I have ever done, and the wisest thing I ever did. We are one in nature and a moment without you is a moment lost. I love you, sweetheart, and I'm ready to cast off that bowline with you.

"Finally, Jesus. When your mother insisted we name you Jesus, I had my reservations. What a name for a child to bear. I know there were many moments where you probably wished we had named you Mortimer, but your name is perfect. Every parent wishes for their child to do great things in their life. We don't have to wish; we know you will. There has never been a single doubt in our minds.

This shop is nothing more than a starting block for greater things. Know your mom and I couldn't disappear if we wanted to and when times seem hard, we will always be that little voice in your head. And if we can't be there for some reason, know that Mary and Sam will be. Now, go out there and become the greatness that is your destiny. We have and always will love you."

Even though my mother said nothing, I looked over and she had a proud smile of accomplishment on her face. Though she probably didn't know all that was going on, she seemed to know that none of it would have happened if it wasn't for her.

Mary's party was a huge success. Everyone was laughing, drinking, and eating the finger foods from Ana's restaurant, but the time was upon us to make our departure. As we were gathering our stuff, Sam came over and whispered in my ear, "You guys were perfect. I knew I chose the right person for the job. It's time for you two to sit back and watch. You will always be my favorite barber."

I wasn't sure what he meant by that, but before I could ask him, I heard Jesus call me, "Dad, are you sure that car is safe? It's such a wreck!"

Barry: "We'll be okay, son. Nothing can go wrong? And if it does break down, I promise we'll figure a way to get to our boat."

We were about to leave, when out of the corner of my eye, I noticed, floating around the room, a big balloon in the shape of a ship with 'Bon Voyage' written on one side and 'Good Luck' on the other.

Barry: "Who brought the balloon?"

Sam: "That would be me."

Barry: "Thanks, Sam, you know me, I've never been very sentimental. But, I will treasure it. I would ask you to take good care of our son, but I already know you will."

I looked over at Ana and said, "Sweetheart, can you do me a favor and grab the balloon? I'll make room for it in the back seat."

www.ingramcontent.com/pod-product-compliance
Lightning Source LLC
LaVergne TN
LVHW091930181025
823782LV00039B/271

* 9 7 8 0 9 9 6 7 8 3 9 1 0 *